The Mysteri(

The Mysterious Case

by

John Press

ISBN: 978-1-326-54588-8

PublishNation
www.publishnation.co.uk

Prologue

All that he sees is light – a blinding, yellow, all-consuming light. But he can hear. Oh, yes, he can hear. Laughter, tears, and screams. Gut-wrenching, ear-piercing, primal screams. His screams. Screams that fill the musty room with his agonising pain and utter despair as the blade cuts and stabs again and again and again.

With his life rushing toward its inevitable conclusion he wonders how such evil can ever be stopped … and then, just as he is consumed by the final, eternal darkness, a single word forms, suddenly and unexpectedly, in his mind …

'Homes …'

Chapter 1

The Incident

My eyes snap open with an audible pop as I'm instantly gripped by a feverish excitement, and I start sniggering like some sort of evil genius! Still, if I can't act like a deranged supervillain today, then when can I?

The reason? Simple. It's the twelfth birthday of none other than the awesome, the amazing – the not at all modest – Susan Queen! And to celebrate this momentous event my dad Bill and my mum Rachel are allowing me to fulfil my long-held ambition of visiting the local kennels and adopting a dog!

Just as I'm contemplating the day and attempting to get my snickering under control a soft tapping at my bedroom door grabs my attention.

"Who is it?" I ask, as if I don't know.

Suddenly the door is flung open and smacks itself against the wall. A couple of cuddly toys wobble precariously on a nearby shelf, but somehow manage to cling on. Unfortunately the same can't be said of Barbie, who I watch tumble gracefully through the air before face planting into an empty crisp packet which is nestling on top of a two-day-old banana skin. This instantly results in Mum and Dad's inevitable lecture about room cleanliness playing in my head like some sort of hideous horror movie.

"Happy birthday, darling!" shouts Mum as she scoots over to my bedside and plants a whopping kiss on my forehead.

"Freeze! This is a police raid," screams Dad. "Anybody with a birthday … don't move, and put your hands out in front of you."

Dad doesn't choose these words by accident. He really is a policeman … and clearly never switches off from work. Ever since leaving school he's been a copper. He started out as a constable on the beat, and he's now a highly decorated detective inspector. If truth be told, he doesn't really talk about his work at home – which is probably just as well, as I imagine that he sees some pretty horrendous sights and has to deal with some very unsavoury characters.

As I struggle with the concept of not moving while putting my hands out in front of me a chocolate cake is thrust into my welcoming arms by Mum. Mum is great. She used to work as a nurse but she gave that up after The Incident, and now works part time in a local charity shop.

I look down at the cake and am confronted by a picture of a dog with floppy ears (icing), a big nose (a chocolate button) and two perfectly circular eyes (Smarties, what else?) who appears to be carrying a very large stick (definitely a Flake). All of this is sitting above the words,

K9 + 3 years old today.

"Thanks, Mum ... thanks, Dad," I chuckle, while contemplating how great birthdays are – the one day a year where I get to gorge myself on chocolate cake for breakfast ... Result!

My parents pile on to my bed, one on either side of me. Mum tries to cut three slices of cake without stabbing me, and Dad tries not to look too keen. He loves his food, as you can see from his ever-expanding waistline and the immense strain that his belt appears to be under.

I can't help thinking that if the belt does eventually admit defeat then it should be given a medal for providing such excellent service under monumental pressure. Even though Dad's trying to hide it I can see the intensity of his stare as he focuses on the cake, and I instinctively know that he's praying with all his might that Mum cuts him a gigantic slab.

Aside from a Smartie that seems to drop off the cake and disappear into the folds of my duvet – I'm sure it'll resurface at some point over the coming week – the cake is cut and enthusiastically eaten while, between bites, we discuss today's visit to Harris's House of Hounds.

Mr and Mrs Harris, along with weekend help from Justine and Calvin – who are earning extra money before uni – run Chalton's premier dogs' home. In truth it's Chalton's only dogs' home, but they've run it with love and care for over twenty years. From time to time, when I was younger, I used to be taken down there for a look around and always seized the opportunity to play with a few of the 'guests'.

Even though I haven't been there for two years it hasn't stopped me from going on and on … and on and on … and on a bit more … about wanting a dog. Eventually Mum and Dad have relented and feel that, at the grand old age of twelve, I'm responsible enough to own man's (and hopefully woman's, too) best friend.

"I can't wait. I'm so excited!" I cry, while simultaneously gently bouncing up and down in bed and watching Mum try to keep her slice – plus the remainder of the cake – relatively stable.

"You deserve this," exclaims Mum, and I watch a tiny tear escape from the corner of her left eye and leave a trail of moisture down her face.

"It's just so unfair what's happened to you!" she shrieks as she smacks down a fist – on to the cake, unfortunately – which creates a tsunami of sponge and icing flying in all directions.

I'm pretty sure I see the dog's nose hit the windowsill. I definitely see Dad's mouth open in the hope of catching any residual confectionery that travels into his vicinity and – worst of all – I see the Flake slamming like a battering ram into the side of last night's glass of water, thus sending a cascade of liquid over my recently completed maths homework.

Even as the last drop trickles from the lip of the glass various excuses to my teacher begin to form in my mind. These range from very localised flooding to mugging by a particularly malicious pod of dolphins.

As you've probably realised by now, I haven't told you everything that you need to know about me. So here goes …

Two years ago, as I was meandering my way home from school, I heard a screech of tyres. I started to turn, and then found myself flying through the air like Supergirl before crashing back down to earth and finding that my life had changed forever.

This is what we in the Queen family refer to as 'The Incident'. Basically, I was the victim of a hit-and-run accident, and my legs are now for ornamental purposes only: they look fine, but quite simply they don't work.

The driver of the car was never caught, and Mum and Dad are still struggling to come to terms with what happened. This leads them to – at times – be consumed with feelings of anger, guilt and powerlessness.

There you go. That's my life laid bare! There are no longer any secrets between us!

We all explode into laughter, and the situation is diffused.

"I'm fine Mum. I'm happy, with the best family in the world. What's done is done."

"You're amazing," sniffles Mum as she eases herself off my bed.

I then imagine the bed breathing a colossal sigh of relief as Dad also removes himself before announcing,

"Now let's get things cleaned up in here, and hit the road!"

Chapter 2

Harris's House of Hounds

One hour and ten minutes later I'm sitting in the back of our Ford Focus, with my trusty chair safely packaged up in the boot. Mum is in the front passenger seat, and Dad has squeezed in behind the wheel.

"Go on, love. Let me use the blues and twos. We'll get there much quicker," he pleads.

"For goodness' sake, Bill, you're off duty. You can't just whack your light on top of the car and career through Chalton for the fun of it," says Mum as she chastises Dad, though she can't help smiling as she says it. "You're just a big kid, aren't you?"

"It's not my fault. I just like the flashing lights and the noise the siren makes," explains Dad, while grinning. "Oh, well … if you won't let me use the real thing then we'll just have to improvise, won't we?"

And so, off we drive, with me and my ever so slightly unhinged family chanting,

"Weee naaah, weee naaah, weee naaah …"

ooOOOOOoo

Fifteen minutes later we turn right into an idyllic tree-lined lane eight miles to the west of Chalton, at the end of which can be found Harris's House of Hounds. As we pull into the car park my eyes flit from side to side as they confirm that everything is still as I remember it.

Straight ahead I spy the Harris's glistening white house, originally built in the 1930s and adorned with an arch of deep pink roses skilfully trained up and around the front door. To the left of the house lies a gate that I know leads to a maze of kennel-lined paths and a large green field beyond, where the dogs can run and play to their heart's content.

An enormous grin spreads across my face as I push open the car door and my ears are assailed by the noise of excited yapping and barking. I didn't think it was possible, but somehow the sights and sounds have raised my feelings of excitement to a level that I previously would have felt were unachievable!

Mum and Dad immediately do the usual grappling to get my wheelchair out of the back of the car and me settled into it. Just as Dad is about to use the sort of language that I would get sent to my room for – one rule for adults and one rule for kids, right? – Mr and Mrs Harris appear. Dad bites his lip, and introductions and explanations are made. By the time all of this has happened I'm set, and raring to get started.

Mrs Harris turns to me with a sparkle in her eye and says,

"It's always exciting to pair one of our dogs with a loving owner. Follow me, Susan, into my Aladdin's cave of canine delights. We have something for everyone, so I'm sure that you won't be disappointed."

ooOOOOoo

Unfortunately, one hour later Dad exclaims,

"I can't believe that you're disappointed!"

I'm afraid to say that he's right. I've seen spaniels sitting, beagles bouncing, and collies cartwheeling (OK, so I'm prone to exaggeration) ... I've dabbled with a dachshund, I've laughed with a Labrador, I've even spoken French with a bichon frise, but none of them wowed me.

Mum has always said to me that when you meet someone you love you'll just know ... and I thought it would be the same with a dog. Don't get me wrong, they were lovely, playful, licky and all around ... doggy ... but they didn't make me feel something amazing inside.

I try hard not to let my shoulders slump, but can't stop my bottom lip from quivering like a jelly on top of a washing machine. 'Aaaagghh' I scream to myself in frustration. It's my birthday. I deserve a wonder dog!

"I'm really sorry, Susan," says Mr Harris as he wrings his hands, "but I just don't know what to say. You've seen all that we have to offer."

"Well, there is …" mumbles Mrs Harris.

"No, we couldn't possibly …" replies Mr Harris.

"But at some point someone's going to have to …"

"I doubt that very much. No. It's ridiculous."

"What's ridiculous?" I enquire, as my interest has been aroused.

"Mmm … well, yes, you see …" stutters Mr Harris, "we do have one other dog, but he's … well … he's been here for four years now, and no one has taken him home."

"Oh, bless him, poor little mite," says Mum. "No one's wanted him for four years."

"Er, that's not quite true," replies Mrs Harris. "Plenty of people have wanted to take him home. It's just that … it's because … it's …"

"It's because *he* rejects *them!*" screams Mr Harris. "He's been here for four long, insufferable years, and he just won't go!"

I can't help but laugh, as Mr and Mrs Harris's collective blood pressure seems to be visibly rising. Any animal that can get them this agitated has surely got to be worth a look!

"Please Mum … Dad … Can we at least see this other dog …? Pretty please … I am the birthday girl, after all."

Dad then makes, possibly, the most ill-fated comment in history.

"Go on, then. What harm can it do? Lead on, Mr and Mrs Harris."

"Justine," calls Mrs Harris to the teenage girl walking past carrying a sack of what I have to assume

Welcome, Susan Queen. It is a pleasure to meet you ... and happy birthday, by the way.

I gasp.

"That's impossible. Dogs can't communicate. And ... and how do you know who I am? And how can you possibly know it's my birthday?"

Quite simple. The significant volume of chocolate that appears to be clinging to your hair – which gives me the impression of communicating with a small blonde gateau – tells me that you have eaten cake already this morning, and we all know that cake is only consumed for breakfast on special occasions ... and, judging by your age, a birthday seems the most logical conclusion.

I deduce that you are Susan because you are wearing a necklace that says 'Susan' in silver lettering. Therefore, unless you are impersonating someone else – or are a particularly bold thief – then this is probably your necklace and your name.

Finally, as for your surname, I have to assume that you are the daughter of this corpulent gentleman – who I happen to know is Detective Inspector William Queen.

"OMG. That is amazing. Dad, how does Homes know you? And what does 'corpulent' mean?"

Obese, lardy, salad dodger ...

"Yes ... Thank you, Homes," Mr Harris interjects.

... Doughboy, fatso, whale man ...

"Homes ... enough!" shouts Mrs Harris.

Apologies. I was simply seeking to provide an answer to Susan's enquiry.

"Don't worry," I cry through my tears of laughter. "My dad's thick-skinned." At which point my Mum and I crack up, and even my Dad can't help chuckling away.

Once my Dad's face has resumed its normal colour – he did go pretty red – he pulls the conversation back on track with,

"Actually, love, I've no idea how he knows me."

"Well, our Homes does fancy himself as a bit of a sleuth," Mr Harris explains. "In point of fact he named himself after Sherlock Holmes."

"He named himself?" enquires Mum.

"Yes," replies Mrs Harris. "His original owners (he got too much for them, and they said he had to go) did give him a name, but he didn't care for it."

Do I look like a 'Mr Fluffykins'? Mr Sherlock Holmes is a character for whom I have the utmost respect, so I decided to drop the 'l' - quite simply a waste of a letter ... that, and there's not much space on the tag on my collar - and christen myself 'Homes'.

And when you say, 'He fancies himself as a bit of a sleuth', may I just remind you of the cases that I've solved since I've been here? There've been missing bones, runaway dogs, a robbery by a gang of particularly vicious badgers, your stolen bra, Mrs Harris (or 'The Cup Case', as I like to refer to it)... let alone the work that I do online. Need I go on?

"No, you need not!" shrieks Mrs Harris.

And, while solving these devious crimes, I've found time to carry out wide-ranging experiments to further the science of crime detection. I know how flammable all 173 varieties of dog biscuit are, I can name the paw print of every type of canine known to man, and I can tell exactly what drink someone has consumed just from the smell of their urine ... and that's not something to be sniffed at.

"Oh, God," sobs Mr Harris. "No one's ever going to have him."

And — whenever I can — I try to aid the local police force in their enquiries, particularly when I think they're struggling ... And that, Susan, is how I know your father.

"It's all falling into place. You wouldn't, by any chance, be geniuspaws@pigeonmail.com, would you?" enquires Dad.

"What do you mean, Dad?" I ask, while at the same time pinching myself to check that this is actually real life.

"Well," explains Dad, "over the last couple of years, from time to time, information … hints … ideas to do with particularly baffling crimes … have dropped into our laps. Quite literally, dropped … as in they tend to be on rolled-up pieces of paper that fall from the sky and land in the staff car park. And they're always signed …"

"Don't tell me … geniuspaws@pigeonmail.com?"

"Spot on. We've even had the lab examine the paper for clues, but we've never been able to find anything concrete to help us identify the author."

"And this is you, Homes?" I ask. "Why not just send an email?"

Too easy to trace. I crave anonymity, and wish only to involve myself in cases that stretch my IQ of 170. As such, I use my own delivery system: pigeon mail, or 'P-mail', as I've named it. It's secure, secret, and only slightly dangerous for the recipient if one of the lads happens to drop something nasty along with the message.

"And have Homes's ideas, insights, and suggestions helped?" I giggle.

Homes arches an eyebrow and stares at my dad.

"Er, mmm, er … Well, yes. All right: I can't deny it. Some are quite useful." Homes's eyebrow seems to arch even further.

"All right … most of the information has been incredibly useful … Probably none more so than in helping us to recapture 'Lightning Rod', a light brown rattlesnake who escaped from London Zoo.

We were all out of ideas until someone dropped a photo from the local paper into the station car park. It showed the successful Chalton men's snooker team, who had just clinched victory in the district cup. All four players had great big grins on their faces, though none quite as large as Rod's - he had been masquerading as a cue!"

Allow me to step in, if I may, Inspector. Or perhaps I should call you Bill, as we're nearly family? Rod is now safely back at the zoo and is happy as can be, given that agreement has been reached to allow him out for important matches. Only last week he rattled in his highest-ever break of seventy-two.

"This is just all too weird," mumbles Mum, who seems to have slumped down on to a nearby bench. "Can you talk, Homes?"

Don't be ridiculous. I'm a dog.

"Mum, it's brilliant," I cry. "He's great. Just think: if he comes home with us you'll have lots of fun together when I'm at school and Dad's at work ..."

"That's what I'm afraid of," sighs Mum.

"And with an IQ like that he could help you with those sudoku puzzles you like doing."

Indeed, Mrs Queen ... or Rachel, if I may be so bold? You clearly struggle with numbers. "How do you know this?" I hear you ask. Allow me to elucidate. Firstly, your right index finger is slightly grey from where you flick to the answer page to help you when you get stuck on those sudoku puzzles.

"Naughty Mummy," I say.

"Help," sobs Mum.

Secondly, I notice that your dress says 'size ten' when it would appear to me that it is a fourteen ... and – strangely – the thread around the label seems to be freshly sewn ... and ...

"Please stop typing," groans Mum.

Finally, I notice in articles about Detective Inspector Queen that you are quoted as being in your early forties where, bizarrely, when I was familiarising myself with the members of the local police force and their families I saw that your birth certificate would make you almost fift … "

"Time to go!" screams Mum, and leaps up from the bench like a rocket being launched into space. "There are no dogs here for us. Never mind. There are lots of other kennels. Bill, start the car!"

"Mum … Stop!" I cry. "He's the one. I can feel it."

"Darling," soothes Dad, "she deserves this. He'll be good for her … and I can't deny that he could be useful to me too."

"You're both insane …" mumbles Mum, but I know Dad and I have won. "But if you really, really want him …"

I wheel myself over to Mum and give her a massive hug, which Dad also joins in with until a polite bark draws our attention back to the screen of Homes's iPad.

Er ... hum. May I have a small say in the matter?

"Sorry, Homes," says Dad as he pulls away from our embrace. "We seem to be ignoring your views, don't we?"

While the concept is appealing, I do have three vital criteria that need to be satisfied:

1. A Wi-Fi connection and a wireless printer.

2. Space for my experiments. (A small sob escapes Mum's lips).

3. Susan needs to be able to throw a stick. I may have a massive IQ, but can't help myself. There's nothing like chasing after a piece of wood for no apparent reason, and then returning to be told what a good boy I am.

"Yes, yes, and yes," I shriek. "We have Wi-Fi, and a printer. You can use the corner of my bedroom, and though my legs don't work my arms are like pistons – I'm ... I'm a fantastic stick thrower ... In fact I'm known for it ... In fact I belong to a stick throwers' society ... We 'stickists' like nothing more than ...

Enough. OK, OK, I'm yours. There is an owner's questionnaire that I need you to complete, Susan, but this can be done in the comfort of your – or should I say our? – own home.

We in the Queen family hug, some more reluctantly than others (Mum), and out of the corner of my eye I can't help noticing Mr and Mrs Harris high-fiving each other ... And I'm sure my ears pick up the words 'thank God', 'at last', and 'champagne'.

When the general revelry dies down Mr Harris fumbles with his mass of keys and says,

"Right, Homes. Let's get you out of that cage, then."

But before he's taken two steps I notice a claw zip out of Homes's paw, insert itself into the lock, jiggle about a bit ... and then, with a satisfying click, the door swings slowly open.

"Er, Homes ... have you always been able to open your own cage?" enquires Mrs Harris innocently. "Because all of a sudden I can't help thinking – what with the cases you've solved here, and now hearing about the amazing things you've done with the police – how you never managed to solve our 'Case of the Missing Custard Creams'?"

Some cases are just too complex even for me, Mrs Harris.

Bill, we really should go. We have cases to discuss, and the traffic will become particularly problematical if we don't leave right now!

We immediately follow Homes, who is rapidly accelerating towards the car park … his tiny legs a blur as he attains maximum velocity!

Chapter 3

Welcome Home … s

We arrive home eleven minutes and twenty-four seconds later, having made good time as a result of Homes providing useful suggestions of an optimal route (ably assisted by the satnav function on his tablet) and Dad showing his driving skills off to the new family member. He beams with pleasure as Homes compliments him on his motoring prowess …

Quite impressive, Bill – especially considering how your weight must impact on your reaction times.

Fortunately Dad only reads the bit up to 'Bill', and so opens the front door of our house with a contented smile on his lips and a spring in his step.

The rest of the day is just perfectly normal, and I'm sure it reflects typical days experienced in houses across the country.

Who am I trying to kid? The next few hours are taken up with:

1. Homes and Dad touring the house, with Homes identifying weaknesses within our home security.

2. Homes's excitement at seeing my chemistry kit for ages six plus:

A necessity for an intellect as enquiring as mine.

3. Mum cutting labels out of her clothes, and spending an hour exercising on the treadmill.

4. Homes suggesting that Dad might like to spend some time exercising on the treadmill.

5. An evening meal where Homes watches us eat, while 'discussing' the most effective dissection techniques.

6. Mum, for some reason, developing a nervous eye twitch (strange).

7. Mum and Dad presenting me with a final surprise birthday gift. Dad had sneaked out and bought a dog collar for Homes. The colour is – apparently – deerstalker green, and there is a rather large and glistening silver disc on which is written,

My name is Homes. Please pass me your phone and allow me to text.

8. Me taking Homes out for some stick throwing, where he explains to me his varied approaches to

catching: the pike, the reverse half-somersault, the reverse half-somersault with twist, and the double axel.

ooOOOOOoo

Before turning in for the night I can't help myself. I simply have to ask Homes whether he thinks that he's going to be happy living here with me.

Indeed, Susan. Your stick throwing was all that I'd hoped it would be. Your mother serves first-class dog food – as well as appearing to have a stash of custard cream biscuits, if tonight's afters were anything to go by.

I anticipate some most enthralling discussions with you father, and my basket in the kitchen is most appealing when slumber is required: high-quality wickerwork, a blanket that appears to offer both warmth and comfort, and a pillow to rest my

monumental brain on … and slobber over when I
sleep. All in all, most satisfactory.

Because I have received such positive feedback
from Homes I can't help beaming from ear to ear as I
explain to him that my best friends, Di and Robbie,
are coming over tomorrow, and that I can't wait for
him to meet them.

Excellent news, Susan. I look forward to it with
great anticipation. However, before you go to sleep,
perhaps I could prevail upon you to complete the
questionnaire that I mentioned earlier? I do like to
keep my records up to date, and the importance of
background information cannot be underestimated.

"Of course. No problem," I chuckle as two pieces of
paper are slid towards me and I reach for my trusty
ink pen. Here goes …

OWNER'S QUESTIONNAIRE	
Name	Susan Queen.
Age	12.
Occupation	1. Schoolgirl. 2. Volunteering at Chalton public library every Friday afternoon while the rest of my class are enjoying the delights of PE (not exactly the lesson of my dreams).
Known Associates	Diane 'Di' Cavendish. Classmate, fellow

librarian, and one of my two best friends. Has fiery red hair and an attitude to match. Known as a 'right mouthy cow' at school.

Robert 'Robbie' Cleary. Other best friend. Also classmate and library helper. Loves films, and borrows DVDs from the library. Not the cleverest person you'll ever meet — my teacher says if there was another brain in Robbie's head it would get lonely. Wears trousers that Di refers to as 'shy', on account of them being too embarrassed to meet his shoes.

Ms Forbes.

Library supervisor. Never been married, wears glasses on a chain (a definite fashion no-no), doesn't have any pets, and has never worn a pair of jeans in her life.

Kind, bakes us cakes, and suffers from occasional eruptions from her bottom that are — quite simply — volcanic.

Major Everard Steel. Monocle-wearing school governor, library regular, and old school friend of Ms Forbes.

Ms Forbes says that Major Steel was nicknamed

	'Shovel' at school. Miss Elspeth Hardcastle. Timid, and also an ex-school friend of Ms Forbes. School nickname was 'Mousey'.
Preferred stick throwing arm	Right.

Are you prepared to pick up dog mess? Select from:
  A) Always
  B) Just not the runny ones
  C) Never
	Always.

Preferred brand of ~~dog~~ biscuit	Chocolate digestive.
Any criminal	No criminal record but

record?	*did once run over Basil (my cousin's pet snail) in my chair, and then threw him out of the window before anyone noticed. My cousin thinks that Basil has left to go travelling.*
Any dealings with known criminals?	*There are two library regulars, who we refer to as Vlad and Grigor. They trundle into the library like a pair of armoured tanks — both over six feet tall, both rippling with muscle — and then spend their time hovering*

	around the Crime section. Di believes them to be a pair of Russian hit men working for a dark, secretive, society intent on world domination.
Have you ever been cruel to animals?	Only Basil (see above).
Do you have any enemies?	I'm not too keen on the school bully, Derek 'Big D' Prentice. Also, my cousin may become an enemy if he ever finds out about Basil.

Chapter 4

Watch Out Below

Sunday dawns, and I roll into the front room to see what the rest of the family are up to. I can't get far, however, as every inch of the floor seems to be covered with papers that look a lot like the contents of one of Dad's police files, which I've never been allowed to see … ever! There is Dad poring over various statements and photos and – every so often – passing pages across to Homes, who is also pawing over them.

"Er … morning Dad … Morning, Homes," I say questioningly. "What on earth are you guys up to?"

"Well," says Dad enthusiastically, "I thought that Homes might be able to offer a unique insight into a case that has been baffling us for some time. Some pets have gone missing from the area, and there are rumours of a gang of vicious criminals who perform acts of unspeakable cruelty on the animals that they steal."

"That's awful," I gasp. "Do we have any ideas about who's behind this?"

"We have a name, and that's all. The gang are led by a master criminal who refers to himself as 'Jack the Ripper'. Other than that we have no leads."

Unlike myself who does have a lead ... one that can be attached to my collar. Perhaps after breakfast you could take me out for a short walk, Susan, as I need to ... do a ... You know. I'd suggest a medium-sized bag for the associated pick-up operation.

"Yes, of course, Homes. No problem. Dad, this is dreadful. How are you ever going to catch these monsters?"

"I'm rather hoping that Homes may be able to help," explains Dad.

And, from my point of view, the case both intrigues and angers me. I am more than happy to use my substantial intellect to see if I can be of assistance. I will also reach out to some of my acquaintances, who may provide some useful insights.

"Aaagghhh," I cry as a sudden realisation hits me. "Dad, what if … I mean, could … what if someone tries to steal Homes?"

Rest assured, Susan. As you may have noticed, I am not like other dogs. I am unlikely to put myself in a vulnerable position. Furthermore, although I am diminutive in stature, I have made a study of a number of self-defence techniques. My favourite of these is kendo which, fortunately, involves the use of a very large stick … And if all else fails I can jump up and bite any would-be kidnappers on the …

"Bottoms on seats in the kitchen, please, everyone. It's breakfast time," calls Mum as she pokes her head round the door. At this point we variously sprint (it's Dad and food: what did you expect?), wheel, and trot out of the room.

ooOOOOoo

Four hours later and Homes and I are waiting in my bedroom for our guests to arrive. I can't deny it but I'm fidgeting with excitement, not really concentrating on the game that we're playing … and then, just as Homes is about to type *'checkmate'* for the third time there comes an insistent buzzing from the front door. I immediately know who it is as only Di can ring a doorbell with attitude!

"Susan, Dianne's here!" shouts Mum from the hallway.

"Are you alright Dianne?" I hear her say, followed by a muttered, "Because you soon won't be," and then, back in her normal voice, "Go on through."

Ten seconds later Di has pushed open my bedroom door and is standing on the threshold of my room with a perplexed look plastered across her face.

"Whooooaaaaa, Suz, what is that?! There's a rat in your bedroom and he's typ ... "

Good afternoon young lady. Mmmmm, you're an interesting one. Dyed hair - you're actually a brunette - which, judging by the tell-tale styling, has clearly been cut by Casper Coiffeur hairdresser to the stars

... and clothes that appear cheap yet, looking at the thread and the fine quality of tailoring, are actually what is referred to as 'high end'. Your nails are bright orange ... cheap nail polish? I think not! I know 'Satsuma Crush' retailing at £45.60 a bottle when I see it!

"Freak alert! Nutter on the loose! This is all rubbish! I'm just an ordinary girl ... "

From an eight bedroom house ... with, judging by the single, chestnut brown, hair on your boot (£120 per pair by the way), at least one horse!

"Not my horse! It's Frank's horse ... he's ... "

Your butler!! Rich girl!

"Aaaagghhh, I'm ordinary, honest Suz ... "

"Oh Di!" I laugh, "I always thought it a bit weird that you never invited us round to your house ... "

I believe that 'estate' is actually a far more accurate description.

" ... Or that you never really knew what I was talking about when I said I queued to get on Easyjet."

No queues on a private jet.

"Does your dad really work for a company that makes dairy products?"

In point of fact, I think that you'll find he owns it. Hence the reason why he is known by his employees as 'The Big Cheese'!

"Yes alright! I'm a rich freak! Everyone'll hate me now!"

"Of course we don't hate you! You're still Di," I laugh, "you're still a wonderful friend and I love you! And you like her too don't you Homes?"

Indeed! You can tell Kim Kardashian over there that I like her very much and her skills in the art of disguise and subterfuge are to be admired!

"Oh Suz, you're the best ... and you, rat-dog, I guess you're kinda cool in a seriously freaky way!"

Just as Di and I have a quick hug we hear a knocking coming from the front door.

"Here he is!" chuckles Di, "Good old Robbie, only he could knock when there's a perfectly good door-bell!"

"Afternoon Robert," we hear Dad say, followed by "Oh dear!"

"Oh dear indeed!" exclaims Robbie as he enters my bedroom, "Look at the state of me! A bird pooped on me just as I was walking up the path!"

Di and I laugh, "These things happen," I say.

"Yeah, but I never heard a pigeon say 'be lucky son' while they were doing it! Nice hamster by the way."

"Robbie!" I exclaim "That's no hamster! That's Homes he's ... "

Irrelevant! Susan, we need to make our way to the back garden immediately! It would appear that the 'Regulars' have arrived!

With bemused looks we make our way to the back door. Homes takes the lead with the rest of us trailing along in his wake, and I grab the opportunity to rapidly explain recent events (by which I mean Homes!) to a dazed Robbie.

As the back door swings open, the first thing that I hear is an "Attttentioooon!" followed by my eyes focussing on two pigeons, their chests puffed out to the point of potential explosion, each with a small black box securely fastened about their neck.

"Good afternoon Mr 'omes sir! Regulars reporting for duty sir! Got your message about your new address sir!" shouts the first pigeon.

"Homes, I've got to be honest, you've taken me a little by surprise over the last twenty-four hours ... but this has taken weird to a whole new level. The pigeon is speaking!"

Yes ... but then again no Susan. He is actually speaking in his standard pigeon dialect but the small box about his neck interprets the movement of his vocal chords and translates this into what you think of as speech. The box was developed by Professor Julius Von Kanderstegg as a favour to me after I helped him locate the whereabouts of his child's toy chimpanzee which had, mysteriously, gone missing. I immediately suspected some monkey business and cracked 'The Case of the Absent Ape' in a couple of days.

"And you did this from within the dog's home?" enquires Di, joining in the madness.

Oh yes, it was elementary.

Anyway, enough of reliving past glories. Susan, Dianne, Robert please allow me to introduce Wing Commander Peters. It's good to see you and the lads again Wing Commander.

"And it gladdens me 'art to see you too Mr 'omes sir. You called, we answered. Always 'appy to 'elp. It's a right pleasure to meet you too ladies ... and you son ... sorry about the ... you know ... we can't help it see ... we're pigeons ... it's what we do ... sometimes it's deliberate but sometimes they just slip out ... and last night we had some of them there blueberries and now it's 'oops there goes another one' and ...

"Honestly, no harm done," says Robbie, "it's all in the past."

"As well as being in your hair!" laughs Di.

"Anyway ... " I say, trying to regain control of the situation, "it's a pleasure to meet you Wing Commander and, I have to ask, why are you called the 'Regulars'?"

"Well you see miss, it's like this ... we's pigeons see and we're ... well ... you know ... regular in our 'abits ... regular as clockwork like. A poop here, a splodge there and sometimes a berry surprise ... do you see what I'm getting at miss?"

"Oh yes!" I laugh, "I'm receiving you loud and clear Wing Commander!" I turn to Robbie and Di – one looking suitably bemused and the other chuckling away – and give them a subtle wink.

"And, pigeon number two, you are ... ?" asks Di turning her attention to the left of the Wing Commander.

"Ho ho! 'Number two'! Very good miss, very good indeed! We pigeons do like a bit of that there toilet humour! I'm very pleased to meet you all, certainly I am. S.C. at your service maaam!"

"S.C.?" I ask tentatively, unsure of whether I want to hear the answer or not.

"Well, 'ere's the thing miss, it's 'ow us Regulars met Mr 'omes 'ere. Ever 'ear of that celebrity chef, Oliver Onion?" begins S.C. We all nod, "Well, 'e opened this new restaurant in London, right posh place it was too and 'e ... well 'e ... 'e wanted ... "

"Come on man pull yourself together, spit it out!" barks Wing Commander Peters.

"Sorry chief, ladies and gent. I get all emotional like, even now. Well, this Onion fella 'e wants to serve ... to serve ... PIGEON PIE!

There it is, I've said it, I feel so much better now! Anyway, so, for this pie 'e needs pigeons don't 'e! And well, there I was, mindin' me own business in Trafalgar square ... just done a corker right on the 'ead of a French tourist, and next thing I know there's a net over me bonce and I'm being carted off with nothing to look forward to apart from forty-five minutes in the oven at gas mark seven!"

"And I, of course, couldn't leave one of me squadron to suffer such a terrible fate," explains the Wing Commander, "I'd 'eard about Mr 'omes 'ere and so approached 'im to ask for 'is 'elp like to rescue me lad."

I was, of course, happy to assist. By vigorously trawling the internet and sending a number of cunning emails I tracked Onion to his lair and then the lads swooped in for a daring rescue raid.

"And swoop we did sir!" snaps the Wing Commander, "In and out we was like greased lightning and S.C. was returned safely to the fold! Job done, mission accomplished, back of the net!"

"Hurrah!" A chorus of approval seems to echo around the garden.

Me, Di and Robbie twist our necks in a variety of directions to see if we can identify the source of this impromptu cheering until our eyes eventually settle on the roof of my house where there are six additional pigeons ... waving at us enthusiastically!

"Excuse the lads ladies and gents, they do get so excited about that there story!" explains the Wing Commander.

"And I have to ask," I interject, "S.C stands for ... ?"

"Short Crust miss! As in the pastry! It's on account of me being minutes from being the main attraction in that there Onion's pie."

"Of course! Silly me! I should have known!" I say in an, ever so slightly, crazed voice, "and ... Oliver Onion ... what happened to him?"

"The restaurant was a great success!" explains the Wing Commander "Probably on account of all the good luck we gave 'im, eh S.C?"

"Too right sir. They say a pigeon pooing on you is good luck ... and we made sure he was one lucky man! Covered from 'ead to toe in good luck 'e was!

Ended up making the restaurant one of them vegetarian eateries and 'as been laughing all the way to the bank ever since! Always wears an 'at now though ... it's become a bit of a ... what-do-you-call-it sir?"

"Trademark"

"That's it, a trademark! Which is much better than a skid ma ... "

"Excellent! Right! Marvellous!" I say, leaping in, "Wonderful background, a pleasure to meet you all but, we'd better get to the business at hand, or wing, or paw ... what brings you here?"

Allow me. You will remember Susan that I explained to your father that I would reach out to some of my contacts to see if I could garner any information about this 'Jack the Ripper' character ...

At which point, Homes is interrupted by furious cooing, squawking and general mayhem from the pigeons on the roof of the house. Even S.C. and the Wing Commander seem to be hopping frantically from foot to foot.

So, I judge from your reaction that you have heard of this individual?

"We 'ave that sir!" replies the Wing Commander, "Just rumours like, but there's an undercurrent of fear starting to spread sir.

Word is that this 'Ripper' steals animals and does 'orrible stuff to 'em. No definite proof, but there was a guinea pig over Brompton way mysteriously vanished from 'is ball in the garden, a rabbit belonging to that magician fella in Westhaven – one minute 'e was there, next minute 'e was gone -, there was a goldfish who seems to 'ave evaporated – I mean, it's blinkin 'ard to accidentally lose one from a glass bowl, and there's been a loada squirrels vanishing – the squirrel community are going nuts about it! It's a real worry. A right old 'bowel wobbler' as they say."

"Ooops! You're not wrong there sir!" shouts S.C.

"Sorry about that miss, gets me right churned up inside this all does and I couldn't help meself! Still, you're mum's roses should come up lovely!"

Right, the game is definitely afoot! If the police are investigating and you lads are hearing things like this then there is, most certainly, a menace lurking which must be stopped at all costs! I, Homes, must find this 'Ripper' character. Lads, you need to be my eyes and ears on this – any news you hear, the smallest rumour, any information at all, you must come to me immediately! Immediately do you hear?

"Absolutely Mr 'omes sir. We're all over it as they say!" barks the Wing Commander, "and it right gladdens me 'eart to know that you're on the case! Leave it with us ... we'll be back! See you soon Mr 'omes and right nice to meet you three. Be lucky!"

And with that, the Wing Commander, S.C. and the other squadron members rise into the sky, arc away over the chimneys and rooftops, off to investigate ... as well as to spread a little bit of luck wherever they go!

"Annnnnnnnd relax ... " says Di breathing out. "That was ... different ... but, then again ... the whole day is starting to feel different ... in fact, I'm not entirely sure that life's ever going to be quite the same again! You alright space boy, you've been very quiet?"

"Absolutely," mutters Robbie, "I mean, what could be more normal than a typing dog and talking pigeons! Actually, I think a little lie down would do me the world of good!"

"Don't worry about it Robbo, come with Auntie Di and Auntie Susan, we'll explain everything over a nice slice of birthday cake!"

Would anyone care to participate in a few minutes of exercise designed to strengthen one's arm muscles? I would recommend some vigorous stick throwing!

Unfortunately for Homes we've already turned around and are making our way back inside for a chat, cake and the beginning of a quiet remarkable few days ...

Chapter 5

Cops and Rob ... bers

With a bit more vigour than usual I push myself back up the front path after setting a new personal best time for my return journey from Chalton High. As you might have gathered, today, I'm keener than normal to make it home to find out how Homes and Mum have got on together on their first day of Mum/dog bonding!

"Yoohoo, I'm home!" I cry as I swing open the front door and remove my key from the - deliberately lower than usual - keyhole.

"Oooohhhhhh gooodie, youssssssh, home shweetiepopee pie," gurgles Mum as she swerves out of the front room before leaning against the door frame " ... and how was your day at schooool, was it lovbeee ... hic?"

"Er, yeah Mum, it was fine," I manage in a slightly bemused tone,

"Robbie wasn't around in the afternoon and we saw a police car out of the classroom window – no idea what that was about - but otherwise, all good. Have you had an enjoyable day with Homes?"

"God! Hic ... I mean good! Yes lovvvey, all hic good! Jusssht a couple of tinsy winsy explosions coming from your bedroom, what seemed to be a talking pigeonsy, hic and a lovely game of ssshhhhticksy poos in the garden ... and some poosy sticks to pick up too! Ha! Lovely, normal, day, can't wait for more, hic! Jusssht off for a teensy weensy lie down ... "

And, with that, Mum pin-balls off down the corridor and half turns half falls into her bedroom.

Whilst my brain searches through its data banks to work out the last time that I'd seen Mum ... well ... drunk, there comes the patter of small paws and Homes rounds the corner.

Greetings Susan, an excellent day of education I trust?

Yup, terrific thanks Homes. Homes, are you wearing glasses?

I prefer to think of them as protective goggles which your mother kindly made for me using three straws and two plastic lids – quite effective as it happens ... and indeed essential when working with combustible materials.

"So," I say, gathering myself, "your day's been OK then?"

Most satisfactory I must say!

Wing Commander Peters popped by ... or should I say 'pooped' by (my little joke) with some most useful data and my experimentation into the explosive properties of digestive biscuits is progressing at a pace!

"Crumbs!" I exclaim.

Indeed Susan, absolutely everywhere in fact. Still, a small price to pay for scientific advancement and I'm certain that, after a couple of washes, your curtains will be as good as new.

I do, however, have some bad news ... Susan, my deductive powers have led me to believe that your mother may be ... an alcoholic!

"No Homes," I laugh, "I think it's just that she's ... "

A boozer, a juicer, on the sauce, under the table, three sheets to the wind ...

" ... struggling to get used to someone new and ... different ... in the house."

I will trust your judgement on this Susan but felt that I should give voice (well, type) to my concerns. Where's the wino now?

"Homes!" I cry, "She's just having a little lie down, she'll be ok, honest. Now why don't you show me what you've been up to?" I inwardly groan and make a mental note about speaking to Dad about where to best hide his wine bottles as I follow Homes into what may, or may not, still be my bedroom ...

ooOOOOoo

During the course of the next couple of hours, whilst I wait for Dad to return home:

1. I clean most of my bedroom

2. I complete my homework – admittedly with some help from Homes - who'd have thought he knew French (*I dated a French poodle for a while*) or, indeed so much about space travel (*it's hardly rocket science*).

3. I find some paracetamol for Mum (*I did warn you – she can get professional counselling you know.*)

4. I realise that I need to cook myself a meal. Homes kindly offers to share his 'meaty chunks in a wholesome jelly' and suggests a 'custard cream binge' for afters. As much as I appreciate his thoughtfulness I decide to grill, or rather, incinerate, three fish fingers – Homes's offer suddenly seeming quite appealing as I look down at the three blackened

rods of charcoal staring, mockingly, up at me from my plate.

Eventually, Dad returns home. No sooner is he through the door than he is confronted with a range of differing welcomes ...

Greetings Bill! A successful day's crime fighting? Is there anything that you wish to discuss?

"Hiya Dad! Good day? Mum's just having a little lie down."

"Yoooo, hoooo, wotcha handsome! Do you love meeee, hic?"

"Wow, what a welcome! First of all, here's a big kiss for my little girl."

"Thanks Dad," I laugh.

"What about meeeee, hic ... lover boy?"

"Yes, a big kiss for you too ... I haven't seen you like this since Ibiza twenty years ago!"

Please feel free not place your lips on my person Bill!

"Thank you Homes," smiles Dad, "and in answer to your question, it's been a tough day and I do need to speak to you ... all of you in fact ... about something rather unpleasant that's happened."

With that we wheel, trot and crawl (Mum, what are you like!) behind Dad into the front room and position ourselves facing him while he leans against the fireplace.

Truth be told, I'm starting to get worried now, Dad's got his serious face on, something that I don't see often and haven't, in fact, since I used a rude word when we were playing Monopoly and I got carried away in the heat of the action - Mum did land on my hotel in Pall Mall no matter what she says!

"You see," begins Dad sternly, "we received a call from your school today Susan because Miss Shakespeare ... " (awesome name for our English teacher) " ... had her purse stolen from her bag."

"Aha!" I cry, "I said I noticed a police car!"

"Indeed. Well, we spoke to Miss Shakespeare and spent some time investigating the crime. Unbeknownst to you students we carried out an extensive search of the premises using three policemen and a sniffer dog called Brutus ... "

A most excellent hound ... smells of sausage, mash and onion gravy.

" ... and we discovered the thief ... "

Tea-leaf, pincher, bandit, looter, pirate, burglar ...

"Rob."

I think you mean RobBER but, yes, that's another, along with ...

"No guys, I mean the thief was Robbie he ... "

At this point, there is an eruption of shouting and furious typing.

"Dad, that is laughable, no way!"

"Nicshh wittle Robbie, nah ... heeessh loveee ... "

He may be on a plane of intelligence well below mine, but even so, he doesn't display any of the attributes that make me place him amongst the criminal fraternity.

"Well," Dad cries, raising his hands to regain some form of order, "that's as maybe but, the purse was found in his bag and he has been arrested and taken down to the station."

"Sssshhhh nice, is he going on a train trip somewhere? Hic!"

"Right," I say, squaring my shoulders, "I need to get round to Robbie's house as fast as possible. He's ..."

A thieving criminal?

"No Homes! He's my friend and he needs my support. As far as I'm concerned it's innocent until proven guilty!"

True Susan ... though, interestingly, recent statistics do show that in 90% of cases ...

"Homes, enough!" I snap "I'm texting Di and she and I will get round there and give Robbie our full support." My fingers flash over the keys of my phone and I provide Di with a brief summary of what Dad has told us.

I will come along also, if I may. I'm known for my sympathy.

I raise an eyebrow whilst my other eye scans Di's brief reply of shocked disbelief and confirmation that she'll meet myself and Homes round at Robbie's.

ooOOOOOoo

Thirty minutes later I roll up to Robbie's front door accompanied by Homes. We've been fairly quick, only needing to 'visit' four trees on the way. We've just about reached the end of the front path when my ears hear the gate creak open behind us and a familiar voice call out, "Hold up, I'm here babe. Wotcha scruff bag."

Good evening ... duchess.

With that, accompanied by a muttered, "I'm really not that posh," Di raises her fist and knocks on the front door. We're greeted by a gaunt looking Mr and Mrs Cleary. Mrs Cleary has clearly (and that's not easy to say!) been crying.

"We just don't know what to do ... he insists he's innocent but has no idea what's happened ... and ... and Mr Cunningham, the headmaster, has said that he's got no choice but to expel Robbie." snuffles Mrs Cleary mournfully.

"Anyway," says Mr Cleary gathering himself, "thank you for coming, you're good friends ... and I'm sure bringing along your pet gerbil will bring a smile to his lips."

Homes, fortunately stays silent as we're led through a short passageway to Robbie's bedroom. The door swings open and reveals him sitting on a dark wooden chair staring vacantly ahead. We rush in as quickly as our feet, wheels and paws allow us and mob him! I hug him, Di hugs him and even Homes shows his human side (is it possible for a dog to have a human side?) by giving him a few quick licks.

Once Robbie has had a little sniffle and expressed his gratitude for us coming round we settle down for a serious discussion. Di sits on the bed and Robbie remains in his chair whilst, simultaneously, tickling Homes under his chin and pulling his ears.

Robbie sets about talking us through his day, which he felt was perfectly normal until he was, without warning, called out of class ...

" ... and I was confronted by three policemen, a dog the size of a horse and your dad Suz. Next thing I know I'm down at the station and I'm accused of being a thief. I was so humiliated!"

I sympathise Robert. Despite my awesome brainpower, I too suffer humiliation on a daily basis –

imagine what it's like for a dog like me – I'm constantly naked and have to greet other canines by sticking my nose up against their hind quarters!

"I'd never do something like that!" sobs Robbie quietly.

I should hope not. At times the stench from those backsides is unimaginable.

"I think Robbie was referring to stealing the purse," I quickly clarify.

Get a grip Robert!

"Homes!" I shout, "That's not fair, Robbie has every right to be upset."

No, I mean his hand keeps slipping off my ear! Grip it firmly and then ... ooooooohhh, that's it! Lovely!

"Come on Rob," let's watch a DVD and chill for bit," suggests Di.

82

"No! I hate DVDs!" screams Robbie.

"OK, OK Rob," soothes Di, "I know things look bad, but we can work this out."

Indeed. Allow me. Robert, are you guilty of this crime?

"No! I'm a pasty!"

I think you mean that you are being framed, which would, in point of fact, make you a 'patsy' as opposed to a pasty which is a large piece of pastry enclosing minced beef and potato, commonly eaten in Cornwall. So, you've been set up. Questions that immediately come to mind are:

Was anything else added to, or indeed taken from, your bag?

"No! No books, no DVDs, no pencils, no pens, no DVDs, nothing."

Has anything occurred recently that you feel may be connected with today's events?

"Not that I can think of. No."

There have been no threats daubed in blood on the outside of your home?

"No!"

No fingers received in the post as a chilling reminder of your past sins?

"No!"

Any toes?

"No!"

Ears?

"No, no body parts of any kind!"

Do you work for the CIA?

"What, the Chalton Ice-hockey Association?"

I refer, in fact, to the Central Intelligence ... no, I think I can safely surmise that this is a 'no'. How about the Secret Service?

"No!"

Have you had any dealings with the Mafia?

"No! No! No!"

So nothing out of the ordinary has happened whatsoever?

"No ... well, Derek Prentice said that I'd get what's coming to me."

"What? When was this?" snarls Di.

"When I arrived at school first thing this morning."

"Right, that's it. The plan is we snatch him on his way to school, take him to a deserted warehouse and slowly and excruciatingly painfully slice bits off him until he confesses!"

Appealing as that sounds Dianne, we cannot take such a course of action. We do not know for certain that this boy is guilty. We need to be subtle and cunning. When confronting such individuals one needs to, first, fully understand their 'modus operandi'.

"Their what?" asks Robbie.

I refer to their method of operation. That is to say, how they behave, the actions that they take and so on.

"Let's put it this way," snaps Di whilst furiously grinding her teeth, "he's a nasty, evil, vile, slimy, greasy, smelly, snotty-nosed ... "

I believe that I am clear in terms of your strength of feeling Diane, but hard facts if you please!

"OK super-brain, you win!" replies Di grinning.

"Basically it's the usual bully-boy stuff: forcing kids to hand over sweets, tripping people up in the playground, making the 'nerds' do his homework for him and his signature move, the 'Big 'D' wash and blow dry!"

"Which," interrupts Robbie, "involves shoving someone's head down the bog, pulling the chain and then drying their hair under the hand-dryer. Believe me, it wears pretty thin after the third time! It got to the point where I started carrying a small bottle of shampoo around with me! I thought that I might as well make the most of it and come up smelling of 'zesty lemon' as opposed to coming up smelling of..."

Yes! Thank you! I believe that I now have the full picture! No doubt such behaviour leaves Mr Prentice 'flushed' with success and his victims traumatised by a, quite literally, hair-raising experience! However, I doubt very much if he has ever dealt with an adversary quite like me before ...

"I'd certainly agree with you there," murmurs Di.

In short ...

"And you are seriously short!" she laughs.

Yes, thank you countess ... as I say, in short, a plan is required from a master crime buster to ascertain our Mr Prentice's guilt or innocence ... and I have just the thing ...

Chapter 6

The Element of Disguise

3.40pm the next day ...

I quickly and quietly open the front door and gently wheel myself towards my bedroom ...

"Just you wait right there lady!" snaps Mum stepping out into the hallway with Dad trailing in her wake.

"And you, where do you think you're going?" Dad adds. Homes stops, one paw in the air and eyes darting feverishly from side to side.

"Both of you, in the lounge right now! You have got some serious explaining to do!"

Thirty seconds later Homes and I are facing Mum and Dad who are sitting next to each other on the sofa. I can tell by their body language - backs ramrod straight, eyes boring into us like lasers - that this conversation isn't going to go well.

"So," begins Mum, "we've had Mr Cunningham on the phone, and I have to say, I for one am fascinated to know about the American student that we currently have staying with us who, and I quote, 'seemed to be very short, had an excess of hair and couldn't speak'! This 'student', it would appear, visited your school today Susan to 'experience life in a typical British school' and ... "

Can I interest you in a drink Rachel? Perhaps a meat pie Bill?

"Do not interrupt me! I'm on a roll here!" screams Mum.

"And she has my full weight behind her!" adds Dad.

Not insubstantial.

"Homes," I whisper, "now is not the time for smart remarks."

Dad puffs out his chest, fixes his eyes on me and says, calmly but sternly, "I think it's time for you to start talking young lady."

OK, I can't deflect them - I need to face the music. A deep breath and here goes ...

ooOOOOoo

8.15 am, 7 hours 35 minutes earlier ...

"Are you sure that this is a good idea?" I ask as last night's brainwave is suddenly feeling very real and decidedly problematical.

Definitely Susan! This is an essential step in ascertaining Robert's innocence. I have spent years studying the art of disguise and feel that I am more than ready!

The four of us are gathered at Robbie's house where Homes is kitted out in sunglasses, a hoodie, jeans and trainers – all fortunately left over from when Robbie was aged three and 'Chuck', the American student, is born. Homes is convinced that he can carry off the character of the 'cool and streetwise' Chuck despite the hoodie proudly displaying the logo 'Bob the builder, can he fix it? Yes he can.'

"Sooooo," I ask slowly, "you've never actually worked undercover before?"

True Susan, but I have no reason to think that there will be any issues whatsoever!

The first issue arises the moment that we leave Robbie's house as Di and I hear a thump and a muffled yelp. We look down to find Homes lying face down in a flowerbed.

Gracious, how you humans walk on two legs I don't know! He quickly types whilst dusting himself down. *Still, I'm sure that I can overcome this minor difficulty.*

With my nerves virtually shredded we make our way to school. I trundle along in my chair with Homes's right paw resting on the chair's arm thus providing enough support for him to totter, somewhat unsteadily, towards our destination.

Eventually we arrive at school, garnering a number of strange looks and whispered comments. But, we have, nevertheless, arrived unscathed.

Game on!

8.40 am ...

I introduce Mrs Hawksmoor, my form tutor, to Chuck an American student staying with us who is keen to experience life in our, typically British, school. I explain that Chuck suffers from a rare growth hormone deficiency and has been mute since birth and so needs to type everything as his preferred way of communicating.

Mrs Hawksmoor politely introduces herself to Homes who then slips effortlessly into the character of Chuck ...

Yo, Mrs H, what's happenin'? High five me girlfriend, don't leave me hangin'!

"Goodness!" laughs Mrs Hawksmoor getting into the swing of things and slapping her hand against Chuck's 'hand', "Good to meet you Chuck! My, your hands have an unusual texture!"

Them's the paw ... hands, I mean hands, of an athlete Mrs H! Baseball's my game babe - I just love holding that great big stick!

9.00 am ...

We enter the main hall for assembly where students sit on the floor facing the front whilst watching Mr Cunningham, the headmaster, deliver his address. Chuck is pulled aside as he is caught scratching his left ear with his hind-leg. Mrs Hawksmoor kindly points out that,

"Whilst the flexibility of your limbs is admirable Chuck, it's not the sort of thing that we find acceptable in an English school."

My bad, Mrs H! Take a chill pill, it won't happen again.

"Er, yes, thank you Chuck ... I think ... "

9.30 am ...

With feelings of panic starting to slowly envelop me, we make our way into Chemistry and find our seats.

"Have any of you seen my custard cream biscuit?" enquires Mr Ibbotson, our teacher.

I gesture to Chuck to wipe the tell-tale crumbs from the end of his nose. Fortunately, Mr Ibbotson is oblivious to our exchange, shakes his head in bewilderment and ploughs on with the lesson.

"Today," he explains, "we are going to perform a practical experiment to investigate the impact of naked flame on magnesium."

This is met with an excited "Oooohhhh" from the class as practical experiments are a rare treat. My insides involuntarily lurch as I spy a twinkle in Chuck's eyes as he envisages an hour of test tube filled excitement.

The class carefully follow Mr Ibbotson's instructions and thoroughly enjoy witnessing the tiny blue flares erupt as magnesium strips interact with the flickering, orange fire.

Without warning, a 'BOOM' echoes around the classroom accompanied by a six foot flame.

Chuck emerges from behind a cloud of dense, billowing smoke and, along with the rest of the class, watches the fire dance across table tops and scamper up walls.

As the resultant evacuation gets underway and I make my way outside, I ponder whether the tightness in my chest could possibly be the onset of a heart-attack.

Who'd have thought using magnesium sulphate rather than the standard magnesium would have such an impact – that's definitely one to watch out for in the future.

"Yes ... Chuck. Perhaps following Mr Ibbotson's instructions might have been the way to avoid attracting attention?"

Indeed. Still, it was quite a pyrotechnic display!

"Mmmmmm." I reply, gently massaging my chest and watching the fire brigade struggle to contain the blaze.

Fortunately, the science block is somewhat removed from the rest of the school and so, after a nervous hour we are led back into the main building.

Mr Ibbotson is being interviewed by a Fire Investigation Officer and I pick up a brief snippet of their conversation ...

"Really officer, I have no idea what happened. It was a perfectly straightforward experiment that I've performed a thousand times before. In all of my years, I've never seen anything like it," explains Mr Ibbotson, his eyes lingering on Chuck as we attempt to sneak past unnoticed.

Back in school, conversation revolves around what has become known as 'Ibbo's Inferno'. Chuck and I chatter along with everyone else and then make a sharp exit as soon as the bell sounds indicating that morning break time has begun.

During break, Chuck concentrates on going for a sniff around and slyly questions other pupils. They seem to enjoy communicating with an American who they think is dressed in a 'retro cool' outfit!

11.30 am

The subject is English and is led by Miss Shakespeare - she of the vanishing purse. My chest, once again, involuntarily tightens as, keen to validate Miss Shakespeare's version of events, Chuck launches into finding answers to questions that he has been itching to ask. There is no subtlety whatsoever as he 'grills' her in the exact same manner as he would an armed bank robber.

Listen up lady, this is serious business and I ain't messin' around so you'd better start singin' like a canary. You dig me?

"Errrrrr ... "

Do you suffer from memory loss?

"Not that I recall!"

Do you have a criminal record?

"Good grief, you Americans are very forthright, but, no, I most certainly do not!"

Have you ever been known to, accidentally, leave things in other people's bags?

"Right, that's it! I don't care for your tone young man – what a ridiculous insinuation!"

Over the course of the lesson Miss Shakespeare is becoming increasing 'miffed' (I can't think why) and, eventually, launches a pencil across the classroom at Jason Maguire who's attention seems to have wandered off down the road and out of the school gates.

Suddenly my eyes are drawn to a ball of fur as Chuck leaps into the air, spins twice, catches the 'stick' in his mouth, lands deftly on the classroom floor and scampers over to Miss Shakespeare.

"Er, thank you Chuck," she says whilst removing the pencil from Chuck's jaws. Her attention is then drawn to what she perceives to be a very strange movement. She sits transfixed as she stares before sternly asking,

"Young man what on earth is going on in your trousers?"

"OMG!" hisses Di from behind me, "He's wagging his tail!"

The lesson ends with Chuck being given a 'verbal warning' - "One more incident and you'll be in front of the headmaster my American friend!"

12.50 p.m. Lunchtime ...

A small crowd is gathered around Chuck due to the novelty of having an American in school along with his uncanny ability to glean details about them and their lives from the smallest of details.

Suddenly, my stress levels start to rise yet again as I notice the approach of Derek Prentice, his malicious eyes focused on Chuck as he draws closer like a lion zeroing in on a zebra. The crowd begins to swell as they sense impending entertainment, with each person feeling an overriding sense of relief that someone else is the object of the bully's attention.

"Well, well, well, what have we here?" drawls Derek, "You must be the famous weirdo dwarf that people are talking about!"

To be fair to Homes, he shows a remarkable sense of self-control as he manages to remain 'in character'.

Yo, what's happenin' dude? You must be the famous toilet dwelling hair stylist ... which is appropriate given how much you look like something that might plop out of my rear end!

A communal gasp arises from the surrounding mob.

"Who do you think you're talking to you American freak!" rages Derek beginning to turn scarlet.

An interesting point (Homes seems to have dropped the Chuck character at this juncture!) *for I believe that I am talking to a 14 year old boy who:*

1. Judging by your pattern of speech refers to his mother as 'mummikins'

2. Has an excess of ear wax

3. On examining the fluff that is clinging to your right cheek, I suspect goes to bed with a cuddly toy fox ... called Reginald!

4. Is wearing - according to my nasal skills - underpants that are, at least, four days old ...

"How could you possibly ... " rages Derek, now turning a worrying shade of purple, "I'm going to kick you so far that you'll end up in orbit you little runt!"

What, in shoes where you've clearly had help tying up the laces?

"Right, that's it you're for it pal, you're so short you couldn't even reach my backside if you jumped!"

At which point Homes proves that Derek's last statement was, in fact, incorrect as with a small growl and a running leap he firmly sinks his teeth into Derek Prentice's right buttock!

"Aagghhh," screams Derek, tears starting to well up in his eyes, "I'll, I'll ... "

"You'll leave him alone is what you'll do!" shouts one of the crowd, clearly feeling bold.

"Yeah," comes another voice, "go home ... and change your pants!"

"I hate you all!" bellows Derek as he starts to run away from the jeering mob.

"That's it," comes a further shout, "turn the other cheek!" At this point any further comments that Derek may have made are drowned out by the combined sounds of laughter and cheering.

"Goodness me!" says Mrs Meekins, the dinner lady, sidling over, "You all seem to be having a good time over here! What's going on?"

"Nothing Mrs Meekins," I answer, still sniggering, "we were just sharing a joke but we're off to the canteen now. Everything's fine."

There is just one thing babe (Homes seems to have slipped back into character).

When we came out to lunch I dropped one of my 'specials' behind that bush over there so you'll need to bag it up. Cheers girlfriend.

2.30 pm

After being sent to the 'reflection room' to have 'a good long think about your actions young man', Chuck is discovered in the school office buried under a mountain of paper which he appears to have pulled out of filing cabinets that he has caused to topple over.

3.30 pm

We leave the school and walk past the burned out husk of the science block with Mr Cunningham's words ringing in our ears. Phrases that made a particular impression included; 'never enter my school again,' 'deported' and 'weird looking kid!'

4.00 pm

"Unbelievable!" mutters Dad, shaking his head.

Mr Queen … Bill … it was important to try to ascertain Robert's innocence and so the character of Chuck was essential in order to …

"Don't Chuck me young man!"

I wouldn't dream of it Bill, at least, not without the aid of a crane to lift your considerable bulk and then as for actually throwing you ...

"Homes, now is not the time," I hiss through gritted teeth.

"Right, just to make it clear, no more detective work," snaps Dad, "and you are both soooo grounded for the foreseeable future! You do not leave this house unless you're going to school!"

Bill, just to clarify, what about when I need to visit your garden to, how shall I put it, 'do my business'?

"Suck it up Chuck!" screams Mum.

Chapter 7

The Truth, the Whole Truth ...

After a rather awkward dinner, Homes and I retreat to my bedroom for a meeting, via Skype, with Di and Robbie – we may be grounded but we can still meet, albeit electronically, to understand whether we've learnt anything as a result of today's events (or 'fiasco', whatever you want to call it) and discuss what we're going to do next.

"Over to you Homes," I say, "aside from ruining any credibility that I had at school, did you learn anything from today's disaster?"

You say 'disaster' Susan, I say master class in deductive reasoning and investigative technique! Allow me to enlighten you all. We now know:

1. Miss Shakespeare seems honest and, I do not believe, is guilty of any deception as far as the 'theft' is concerned

2. Your school dinner ladies have very low standards of hygiene!

3. The other kids at school feel that Chuck is one 'sick' dude - which, I believe is a term of praise and affection!

4. Derek Prentice could not possibly have committed the crime ...

"What!?" Di and I cry simultaneously.

Indeed. Firstly, having met Derek, whilst he is a bully and now has a very sore 'butt-cheek' (I believe this is the term) I do not believe that he has the mental fortitude to commit such an act.

Secondly, and most importantly, my rigorous examination of school records has revealed that Miss Shakespeare has stated that her purse was with her up until morning break and so was stolen at some point after that ... yet Derek Prentice left for an appointment at 10 am and didn't, subsequently, return to school!

"What appointment?" snaps Di.

He was, apparently, having braces fitted.

"Why, did his trousers keep falling down?" asks a baffled Robbie.

No Robert, I think that the braces were being fitted to his teeth.

"Right, wow, I didn't see that one coming," I say, "So Rob, it looks like we need to explore other options."

"No!" screams Robbie suddenly and unexpectedly, "No more detective work! I don't need help from any stuck up rich girl, well meaning cripple or genius ferret! Just leave me ... "

CLICK

Homes's paw cuts the computerised link and comes to rest gently on my hand as I feel my cheeks burning and my eyes begin to fill with tears.

Susan, he is hurting and very afraid. There is something else going on here that we are unaware of – and, whatever it is, is making him lash out at the people he loves. I promise you, he will be filled with remorse almost immediately.

BUZZ ... BUZZ ...

I accept the incoming Skype request and there is Robbie staring at me. "Oh Suz, Di, Homes I'm so, so sorry!"

On occasion, I amaze myself ... Robert, the truth if you please ... what was on the DVD?

"DVD?" exclaim Di and I in unison.

"How could you possibly know?" gasps Robbie.

1. Yesterday you showed considerable agitation when asked if you wished to watch a DVD

2. You mentioned 'DVD' twice when describing things that <u>weren't</u> taken from your school bag

3. You seem traumatised by something over and above a stolen purse

Please enlighten us.

"OK ... OK," says Robbie steadying himself but still finding himself unable to prevent a tear from escaping and rolling down his left cheek,

"I got a DVD out of the library on Friday you see ... and then, Sunday evening, I decided to watch it, opened the case and ... there was nothing in it! 'Weird' I thought, went to put the case back in my bag ... fumbled it ... it fell on to the floor ... the middle section fell out and there, behind it, was a DVD. I thought this was all really peculiar but put the disc into the player all the same and ... and ... it was horrendous ... "

"Take a deep breath Rob, you're doing great" encourages Di.

"There were, there were ... " sobs Robbie, " ... there were animals being cut up and they were alive and screaming and then dying and there were blades and someone laughing and ... it was the worst thing I've ever seen! I can't get the pictures out of my head, I can't sleep at night, I can't think straight. It scared me so much!"

Calm yourself Robert, you've said enough. Clearly, you were not meant to come into possession of that DVD ... something which definitely feels like a serious error by some despicable characters. Could this be the break in the 'Jack the Ripper' case that I've been hoping for? Quite possibly!

Robert, I need to examine this vile DVD immediately! I trust that you still have it?

"Well, you see ... I lied to you!" cries Robbie, "It was in my school bag ... and ... it must have been stolen at the same time that the purse appeared. I noticed it was gone just as those two Russian blokes from the library walked past and one of them said

'Keep your mouth shut little man or it's curtains for you!' I was so worried when the police came that I just didn't know what to do ... which I know isn't unusual for me, but I was all over the place!"

"I knew it!" shouts Di "What were those two stone cold killers doing in the school eh? We're right in the middle of a James Bond plot!"

Ten minutes later, after we've provided more information about Vlad and Grigor to an agitated Homes, Di, myself and Robbie all agree that given current arrest/grounding rules we can't do anything until we're back at the Library on Friday but then ... POW! ... we needed to strike and work out the Russians' devious game.

I concur. I would suggest that I blend in by assuming the role of a small, old lady researching cup cake recipes. All I will need is a scarf, a small skirt, a walking stick and some false teeth.

"No!" cry three voices.

Mmmmm, my expert detective instincts are telling me that you, perhaps, do not favour this approach?

"No way Homes!" I say firmly, "Not after what happened at school. I would suggest you play the role of a small dog belonging to a library helper."

An excellent suggestion and a role that I feel I can play to perfection ... perhaps just the false teeth then? No? I can tell from your faces that that's a 'no'! So be it.

At this point we all decide to turn in for the night. Robbie seems happier now that he's unburdened himself and things are starting to fall into place. All we have to do is:

1. Work out what diabolical scheme two Russian hit men are involved in without getting ourselves killed

2. Tie the above into 'Jack the Ripper'

3. Ensure Robbie gets reinstated into school

4. Get Mum and Dad speaking to me and Homes again

Excellent! Real progress! Who am I kidding?! Still, life's not dull. Roll on Friday ...

Chapter 8

How To Look A Killer In The Eye

The following day I suck in a huge intake of breath as I wheel myself into the house at the end of my first 'post-Chuck' school-day. "Hi everyone, I'm home!" I call out somewhat nervously.

"A good, trouble-free, day at school?" enquires Mum stepping into the hallway. I inwardly sigh with relief as: a) Mum seems to be sober b) she isn't shouting.

"Yup! I was the model student, honest!" I cry and then, whilst simultaneously uttering a short prayer, casually ask,

"Er, how has Homes been today?"

"Mmmmmmm, well I have to say he's been as good as gold. He's spent most of the day holed up in your bedroom and I haven't heard any strange noises coming from there at all. He does seem to be making a real effort – he offered me one of his custard creams earlier which I might well have had if it weren't for the fact that I'd seen him lick it.

Oh yes, and I looked out of the window just after lunch and saw him trying to bag up his own ... 'you-know what' – no easy task when you have to use your teeth! To be honest, I did feel sorry for him and appreciated the effort that he was making so I went out to help him finish the job - if you'll pardon the expression - and then cleaned his mouth for him when he came back in."

"You're the best Mum!" I chuckle.

"I'm glad you say that ... especially as it was your toothbrush that I used."

Despite inwardly grossing out I manage to squeak out a, "Fair enough. I guess I deserved that," before noticing a slight twitch at the corners of Mum's mouth as she turns away and plots a course towards the kitchen – definitely an 'almost-smile'!

"I'm making progress at getting back into her good books," I think to myself as I push open my bedroom door to be confronted by ...

Whoooaaa!! A spider's web of red wool is criss-crossed from one side of my room to the other with scarcely any floor visible!

"Ho ... o ... Homes?" I stutter. In answer to my call I see a tail rise out of the sea of scarlet like a periscope from the ocean. There's a quick double wag and then the tail is gone, immediately followed by the sound of scuffling as Homes makes his way towards me from beneath the mesh. Twenty seconds later his small face emerges.

"Homes, what is all this ... and why are you moving your mouth like that?"

Good afternoon Susan! I am attempting to show you my teeth! I think that you'll agree I've never looked so good! Your mother has done a splendid job and, I must say, has a very steady hand when she is not in the grip of her alcoholism.

"Right ... OK ... marvellous and, yes, you look magnificent. Now, please explain what on earth is going on here?"

Aha! Yes, well, despite being in the dog-house - quite literally in my case - I thought that I would spend my time and massive intellect on looking in more detail at the 'Jack the Ripper' case. I have scoured the internet, including, old newspaper stories and have amalgamated this with information from Wing Commander Peters to form a picture of missing animals and brutality that appears to have been going on, unnoticed, for years!

The red yarn draws a map linking various crimes to the places where they have occurred with different objects representing towns and villages – for instance, 'Cuddly Panda' is Blessingham, your hairbrush is, appropriately, Brushnorton, Ken and Barbie are Upper and Lower Drayburn and so on. By the time that I came to Chalton I was almost out of objects to use but, fortunately, stumbled upon your 'Secret Diary' that you keep concealed at the bottom of your knicker drawer!

"Aaaaaaggggghhhhh" I scream before managing to ask, "Please tell me that you haven't opened it?"

Well no ... ish. When I placed the diary in its allocated position it fell open but, the good news is that I have only read a single page – the one where you explain how much you would like to kiss Kevin Gillespie in Year 8. I take it that your head is in your hands as a result of your love for Mr Gillespie?

Excellent! I have more good news which should make you even happier! During lunchtime I produced a brief 'Potential Boyfriend Questionnaire' which you are free to pass to the man of your dreams – I thought that you'd approve of the question about liking small dogs and the other about ability to hurl pieces of wood.

"Keep breathing!" I tell myself as my pulse rate slowly edges its way back to normal. "Thank you Homes, your efforts on my behalf are great but, changing the subject, do you feel you've made any progress in the hunt for 'Jack the Ripper'?

Definitely! All I will say at this stage is that a picture is emerging and the net is tightening!

"Marvellous, that's music to my ears. By the way, where did all of this wool come from?"

Fortune was smiling on me Susan when I came across an old woollen blanket.

My eyes follow Homes's gaze and come to rest on what remains of Mum's favourite angora wool poncho. "Best not mention this to Mum," I sigh, "at least, not today ... or this week ... or this month ... maybe in about a year's time we'll raise the subject."

ooOOOOoo

Thursday passes without incident. I concentrate on continuing to get on the good side of everybody –

that is to say Mum, Dad and any of the staff at school who felt traumatised by their experiences with a certain American student!

Homes squirrels away on his iPad sending emails, searching a variety of websites and trialling a 'secret' new app that he's downloaded.

Mum notices a few more pigeons than normal in the garden, but doesn't think this at all strange.

At last, Friday dawns and, after a morning of constantly looking at my watch, it's 'Library Time'. Since 'The Incident', the library has been my life-raft in a sea of frustration.

Don't get me wrong, I'm resigned to my life as it is now but, straight afterwards, I wasn't. Life was hard and I struggled to cope with the fact that so many things that I took for granted were doors that were suddenly closed to me. Yes, I tried to keep my chin up and told people 'wheelchair jokes' so they could say, "Wow, Susan's tough, she's just getting on with things and laughs in the face of adversity." But, inside I was angry and consumed with feelings of helplessness and a belief that I had nothing worthwhile to offer.

The library helped me find my way through those dark days and come, relatively unscathed, out the other side. The school allowed me to go and help Ms Forbes, who runs the library, every Friday afternoon ... and I found that I loved it! I learnt about how the library system works, I discovered a love of books that I never knew I had and helping, and chatting to, the 'general public' was, and still is, a joy. In all of this, Ms Forbes was my crutch. She taught me, encouraged me, treated me as an equal, laughed with me, cried with me and, every so often, baked wonderful cakes to share with me. Despite being from a different generation I'm still proud to call her my friend.

Eventually, Di and Robbie were allowed to join me and that was cool – they were my best friends anyway so I was happy to share my Friday afternoon adventure with them. They appear to enjoy it too, even if Di does make out that she gets frustrated with the old people always needing help with the computers. She reckons she once caught one of them trying to feed cheese to the mouse but I'm pretty certain she was joking!

Anyway, on this particular Friday, I arrive first and explain to Ms Forbes that today was 'bring a pet to school day' and that was the reason why Homes was accompanying me. "Hey, that was only a little white lie ... " I mutter to myself.

As opposed to a little white wine in your mother's case!

"Thank you Homes".

Anyway, Ms Forbes seems a little concerned but accepts the situation and even gives Homes a little tickle under the chin which receives a double wag from Homes – praise indeed!

Robbie displays real character by turning up and showing the world that he's not ashamed of what's happened and because he knows that he's innocent.

Last to arrive is Di with a bag bulging in a most peculiar and alarming manner.

"Wotcha gang," she says, "are you carrying?"

"What do you mean 'carrying'?" I ask nervously.

"Oh come on Suz, you know what I mean ... I mean are you tooled up?"

"No I am not!" I cry indignantly, "I don't believe in violence! What in heaven's name have you got in there?" At which point Di opens her bag and brandishes a very large ... wooden spoon.

Excellent Diane, if we are confronted by excessively aggressive behaviour we will stir them into submission.

"It was all Mum and Dad would let me have ... and, even then, only because I said we were doing cookery this morning."

Superb quality of wood though. Still, I'd expect nothing less.

"Homes!" I warn as Di's face darkens. "Look," I say, diffusing the situation, "the plan is we observe and only pounce when the time is right."

And so we all get on with our normal duties, aside from Homes who is, seemingly, wandering aimlessly about, sniffing here, sniffing there and receiving the occasional stroke from Ms Forbes.

A PARP! Suddenly echoes around the library.

Heads down everyone, we're under attack!

"No Homes!" I whisper, "You remember what I said on my questionnaire about Ms. Forbes's 'wind problem'?"

Of course, of course. Still, that was quite something! I actually felt my fur move! The military would pay good money for a weapon like that!

Our conversation is suddenly interrupted by a, "Double vodka in the house!" being whispered by Di as she scoots past. Given this signal we are all suddenly on a heightened state of alert, subtly watching Vlad and Grigor as they move amongst the shelves like a couple of articulated lorries.

After ten minutes, during which my nerves are absolutely shredded, Ms Forbes tells us that she's going out to the back of the library for a quick tea break. We immediately spring into action!

As planned, I rush to Ms Forbes' desk and ask Vlad and Grigor if they could come over, as there appears to be a problem with their library cards. They stroll over, look down to pull in their chairs and then, when they look up again ...

BLAM!

They're blinded by a light shining directly into their eyes (Ms Forbes's desk lamp) with Di, myself, Robbie and Homes carefully positioned behind it. Homes switches on his new app that translates writing to the spoken word. I take notes (which are produced below) while Homes's metallic and slightly robotic voice leads the interview!

Interview commences at 2.23 pm. Those present: myself, Homes, world leading canine detective; Susan Queen, my owner; Dianne Cavendish, rich girl and suspected royalty and Robert Cleary, suspected criminal.

HOMES: Please state your names for the record.

VLAD: I am Kurt

GRIGOR: My name is Karl

HOMES: Where in Russia are you from?

KARL: Ve are German!

HOMES: What is your relationship?

KURT: Ve are business associates ... and vhy is she holding a big spoon?!

DI: Let's see how far you get with your plans for world domination with this monster mixing utensil shoved up your ...

HOMES: Diane, please. Calm yourself.

KURT: Yikes, she is scaring me!

HOMES: There is no need for violence, just slowly lift out your guns.

KARL: Vot guns?

HOMES: I notice a bulge on you right hip that has the exact dimensions of a gun.

KARL: Nein!

DI: Nine guns! My god, that's an arsenal!

KURT: No! Nein is 'no' in German! I mean ve have no guns and ve don't support Arsenal, ve are Manchester Utd. fans!

KARL: Ja! Ze bulge is only a measuring tape. Ve never know when ve vill need to measure up for soft furnishings!

HOMES: What?! Still, I put it to you that on Monday June 11th you threatened this young man.

KURT: Ve see him at school and ve make a little joke, yes?

DI: Threatening to end someone's life is no joke!

HOMES: I quote ... "It's curtains for you."

KARL: Vell yes! Ve vere delivering ze new crushed velvet curtains for ze staffroom! Ve thought zis vas a perfect opportunity for a tiny joke. Zis vould be considered very funny in Germany!

HOMES: Aha! The fog that has surrounded my thinking is lifting! I put it to you that you are also fans of Doctor Who?!

KURT and KARL: Yes!!

DI and ROBBIE: What is going on here!?

HOMES: As I suspected, you do not come to the library to study crime books at all! I have observed that you borrow books from the adjacent section on ... interior design! I noticed a bill at the school from Tardis Interiors - 'We make those small places seem so much larger'. You are Tardis interiors!

A confused mixture of voices as everyone talks at once: Yes ... good grief ... perfect sense ... so sorry ... huge misunderstanding ... zat spoon vould look nice on a vall with a lime green backing and, perhaps, a border of sea shells ...

Things then degenerate into a good natured discussion at the end of which promises are made for the delivery of a rug for Homes which will accentuate his fur colouring and Di has made an appointment for 'the lads' to come up with some designs and colour schemes for her bedroom – everyone agrees that 'black is soooo last year!'

Our revelry is interrupted by Ms Forbes returning from the rear of the library flanked by her old pals Major Steel and Miss Hardcastle.

"Aaaaccchhhooooooo!" sneezes Miss Hardcastle.

"I'm sorry to have to break up the party ladies and gentlemen," states Ms Forbes, "but some work does need to happen at some point this afternoon. Furthermore Susan, I'm afraid that you will need to take little Homes home ... ha, ha, did you see what I did there, ha ... as Elspeth has a terrible allergy to dogs."

I look for Homes and find him lying flat on his back at the feet of Major Steel who, ignoring him, adds "And a library is no place for a hound!"

"Quite." agrees Ms Forbes, "Off you go Susan and I'll see you next week ... preferably unaccompanied by any canines if you please."

"I'll see you guys tomorrow!" I shout as Homes and I depart.

Despite being grounded, I have been allowed to take Homes out for his Saturday walk and so we've agreed to have a sneaky team meeting at the local park.

"Yup, laterz babe" calls Di.

"We need a plan C don't we?" adds Robbie dejectedly.

"Chin up Robster!" I call as I turn right out of the library doors whilst being pulled along by, a decidedly perky, Homes.

ooOOOOOoo

At 10 am the next morning we're all gathered together and I find myself saying, "I've got to admit, I am concerned guys, we're kind of out of ideas here."

On the contrary. The case is all but solved. Robert, your innocence is assured.

"What?!" cries Robbie.

I have cracked the case wide open. In fact, the case is about a case, taken from a case just in case the person who had the case realised they had the case that solved a number of outstanding cases. It wasn't an open and shut case but it's almost case closed!

"You're a total head case!" laughs Di, "Come on then mastermind, out with it."

All in good time, though, suffice it to say, no further doubt exists - this is all linked to that evil individual known as 'Jack the Ripper'! There is now a game that must be played to a conclusion. I have a couple of loose ends to tie up including going back to where it all began ... to where that DVD was first taken from ... the library.

"We can go there now if you like!" I cry.

No Susan, I need to go when no one else is around just to double check that my suspicions are correct.

"How on earth can you do that?" I ask

By calling in specialist help ...

Chapter 9

The Cat That Got the Cream

"I guess that would be me Sugar Chops!"

I look up and behold, perfectly balanced on a branch overhead, a cat with white feet, a white stomach, a black body, a face which is predominantly black but with a white patch over the left eye ... oh, and claws covered in orange nail polish! I look back to Homes, or should I say 'Sugar Chops' and ... yes ... he is ... he's blushing!

Allow me to introduce Irene. Irene is what we call a BAR expert.

"Whoa!" cries Robbie, "You mean she's a sheep impersonator?"

No Robert, she is a <u>B</u>reak-in <u>A</u>nd <u>R</u>etrieval specialist. The best there is in fact.

"You are just totes supapolite Homesy babe! It's, like, mega to meet you all!" purrs Irene surveying us each in turn. You must be Susan – cool wheels girlfriend! You must be Diane – working those Jimmy Choos! ... "

"You said they were from Primark!" I exclaim.

"Yeah ... well ... ." mutters Diane.

"And you ... Robbie," continues Irene, "love the geek chic look!"

"The what?" asks a bemused Robbie.

"Don't sweat it babe, it's just that I'm loving the trouser length – I hear it's healthy to let the air get to your ankles!"

"So, Irene," I say, "it's terrific to meet you and when Homes says you're an expert at break-in and retrieval ... ?"

"My little perfect poochie is being tooooo nice! I've got issues babe ... and I'm trying to face up to them. Bascially, I'm ... a ... klep ... klepto ... kleptomaniac! There, I've said it!"

Excellent progress Irene! Well done!

"What's a klap ... klop ... what's that thing you are then?" enquires Robbie.

"Well, you see babes, it's like this ... " explains Irene jumping down from her perch, landing effortlessly and rubbing up against each of us, "it's

144

like ... I see you've got something nice and the next minute it's, like, mine! Like your Armani watch babe."

Di's eyes shoot to her wrist, "What the ... ? Where ... ?"

"Right here babe!" smirks Irene, dangling the watch that Di had told us was 'just a copy'!

"And you girl! I just love your earrings!"

"No way!" I shriek as Irene unfurls a paw to reveal my favourite, jade, earrings!

"And you Robbie babe ... ." begins Irene.

"My god! You've stolen my pants!" screams Robbie.

" ... I was about to say, I haven't taken anything from you sweet thing."

"Of course, you're right! I forgot to put any on this morning! Phew, what a relief!"

"So, what you're really saying," challenges Di, "is that you're a thief."

"So harsh babes! But, alas, so true! Homsey poos caught me and tagged me with this black box which helps him keep track of me and enables me to speak to you wonderful people. He's also helping me face up to my issues. He's my wonder pooch!"

And you are doing exceptionally well Irene.

Homes so fancies her!

... and Irene helps me, from time to time, because, even I, on occasion, need the aid of an expert cat burglar.

"I get that you're a burglar ... " muses Robbie, " ... but, where does the cat bit come into it?"

A stunned silence settles across the group ...

"So Irene," I say, still shaking my head, "where do you, er, live?"

"Aaaahh babes," sighs Irene, "you've heard of the saying 'the cat that's got the cream'? Well, when you're like me you've usually got the cream but also had it away with the emerald necklace, ruby ring and, in your case Diane, the diamond tiara as well ... and that doesn't make me that popular a pet so I live on my own and on my wits. What's a girl to do eh?

Anyway, moving on ... so, mega-brain, you pigeoned me -I love those boys ... like, well messy ... but a right laugh! - what's the story then?"

With that, Homes, briefly, recounts events to date and explains how he wants to get into the library, out of hours, to investigate certain 'things' that are concerning him.

"Sounds my kind of gig babes! We'll be in, we'll be out and no one will be any the wiser! When do you need me wonder dog?"

Tonight. Time is of the essence!

"Ooooohhh, I love it when you're in charge! My little tiger!"

Good grief! Arrangements are made and, with Homes all gooey eyed and with his tail vibrating so fast that he's in danger of taking off like a helicopter, we all move off in different directions.

My nervousness has been rising steadily over the last few days, and so I ask, "Homes, shouldn't we, perhaps, tell my dad what's going on?"

Definitely Susan. As soon as I've confirmed my suspicions. I need to carry out some further on-line investigations this evening followed by my late night mission with Irene. Rest assured we'll involve the appropriate authorities when the time is right.

"OK if you're sure. You kept Irene quiet … tiger!"

I don't know what you mean Susan! Irene is merely an associate!

"Mmmmmmm … fair enough … "

Thank you. By the way, do you think you'll, perhaps, be able to procure some of your father's aftershave for me to use later?

Chapter 10

Y Are You Dressed Like That?

The moment that I've finished chewing my last mouthful of dinner I ask to be excused and propel myself to my bedroom in order to check on Homes's preparations for his night-time excursion. Truth be told, I'm worried – he's been with us for less than a week and, already, he's heading out on a potentially highly dangerous mission.

As I open my bedroom door my nose is assailed by a strength of odour that I would previously have thought was impossible to achieve.

"Wow!" I exclaim, "How much aftershave did you actually use Homes?"

All of it Susan! I have literally covered my entire body – from the top of my head right down to my 'dingily-dangly'! Do you think that Irene will be impressed?

"I think that I can honestly say that she's never going to forget tonight – and that's probably also true of anyone who happens to be within a mile radius of you."

Excellent! I do like to make an impression!

When I can't hold my breath any longer and I'm seconds from completely blacking out, I suck in another huge gulp of air (mixed in a 50:50 ratio with the aptly titled 'Eye of the Tiger' cologne) and manage to ask, "So, what exactly are you up to?"

Since Irene and I are looking to depart a little later, I have plenty of time to examine a blueprint of the library such that I am completely familiar with the building, or should I say 'lair', that I will be infiltrating. Alongside this I am confirming a suspicion that I have by examining a web-site about ...

"Cockney rhyming slang!" I manage to say as I look over Homes' shoulder between prolonged bouts of breath holding, "What's all that about then?"

I believe that this may actually be an important facet of the case and one which I will reveal when the time is right.

"Fair enough, but what, exactly, is cockney rhyming slang?"

Aha, it is simply a form of speech, developed in the East End of London whereby certain words replace other words with which they rhyme. For instance:

Your father needs to go to the 'Fatboy-Slim' (where 'Fatboy Slim' replaces the word 'gym').

Your mother likes a 'tiddlywink' (where 'tiddlywink' means 'drink').

"O.k, I think I understand!"

Please get off my tail.

"Let me guess! That means ...

You like drinking ale

You'd like to go for a sail

It's blowing a gale

You're going to jail!

You've got email

You ... "

Excellent as your guesses are Susan, what I'm trying to communicate in this instance is that your left tyre is right on top of my tail and it's starting to become excruciatingly painful!

"Oh Homes, I'm so sorry!" I say, edging my chair forward and hearing a little whimper of relief. As I do so, I catch sight of a portion of an email, protruding from beneath Homes' iPad.

"I'm also intrigued by that piece of paper." I say, whilst motioning at the note that I've caught sight of. "Why is someone writing to, if I'm reading it right, 'Longbeech Boarding School' and who's the 'Dr Stu Macacres' who's been doing the writing?"

Well Susan, Dr Stu Macacres is, in point of fact ...

"You!" I cry.

And you know this because ... ?

"Because ... because ... aha! Because Dr Stu Macacres is an anagram of 'custard creams'!"

154

Bravo Susan! Your skills as a detective are developing magnificently!

"Thank you Homes, you're too kind. But, what on earth are you contacting a school for?"

Rest assured Susan, it is all linked to my unmasking of a criminal mastermind and will be revealed in due course.

"Fair enough I guess," I sigh, "Changing the subject then, I have to ask, Homes are you missing the kennels at all? I mean are you happy here with us ... with me? I realise that I'm probably not exactly what you were hoping for as an owner ... "

Susan, rest assured that I'm having a most enjoyable time! I could ask for no more from an owner! You are kind, care deeply about your friends, are prepared to bag up my 'you-know-what', sometimes under the direst of circumstances, and it's

155

been less than a week and already we're in the midst of an excellent adventure!

There's little that I miss about the Harris's or their accommodation. They were nice enough but always found me a little more than they could handle. I enjoyed the Sunday football, but even that was losing its appeal after our keeper, 'Big Angus', found a home and we started leaking goals. A 6-0 trouncing by 'Dorking Dachsunds' was a bitter blow! So, yes Susan, I could not be happier!

"I'm so pleased that you're happy!" I cry enthusiastically whilst, simultaneously, bending down to give Homes a little stroke, "I think that you're terrific!"

Thank you Susan, that is much appreciated. I have to say that you've done very well not to mention the … you know …

"Well, I didn't like to say anything and I wanted to give myself the opportunity to work out the reason for it. So, go on then, why are you wearing a pair of my dad's black Y-fronts on your head?"

I think that you'll find that they're actually 'midnight blue'. The reason, however, is quite simple – by pushing my head through the left leg I have a ready-made balaclava! Even though the library should be deserted, I do not want to run the slightest risk of being identified.

"Very clever," I reply whilst opting not to mention the fact that, despite not being able to recognise Homes from his face, anyone with a functioning nose could, quite literally, identify him from a mile away.

"I'm really worried," I continue, "if you genuinely believe that the library is linked to 'Jack the Ripper' then this is seriously dangerous stuff. So, I'll ask one final time, are you certain that you should be doing this?"

Yes Susan, I am. Terrible cruelty has been going on, unchecked, for years and this is an opportunity to put a stop to all of that suffering. Myself and Irene will be fine I'm sure – we'll crack the case, advise your father and then settle down to plan my birthday.

"Your birthday!" I exclaim, "I should have checked! When is it?"

It's still a fortnight away, so plenty of time.

"Phew! At least there's time for me to buy you a present. Did you have anything in mind?"

A present is not necessary Susan ... though if you were keen to purchase a small gift then I have jotted down one or two ideas.

A printed list is slid towards me and I begin to scan the thirty-five items listed. A few in particular, leap out at me:

A family size pack of custard creams

Test tubes of various sizes

Gun powder (I instantly hear the clink of glass as Mum reaches for a wine bottle)

A false beard (what?!)

Just as I'm contemplating under what circumstances a 'parachute (extra-small)' is likely to be required, my attention is drawn to a light tapping on my bedroom window.

I wheel myself over, undo the latch, open the window and, with a single, graceful bound, Irene leaps in and lands on my carpet as silently as, well, a cat!

"Whoa, babes you smell hot!" purrs Irene, "I caught a whiff from six streets away! Is that scorching scent for me you hunky hound?"

"It's just a little something that I dabbed on – it's nothing really," types Homes, playing it cooler than a penguin in an ice bath.

"Mmmmm, if you say so you cute canine. I'm not sure that 'dabbed' is quite the word to use though. Nice 'Y's by the way – they're seriously big, verging on enormous in fact!"

Indeed. Well, Susan's father is a man of significant girth. Still, they do have the advantage of both concealing my face and keeping the remainder of my body nice and warm. If you feel that you require something similar then I happen to know that Susan owns a pair of knickers that I think would accentuate your eye colouring perfectly.

"Oh Homesy, you're so romantic, but I'll decline if that's OK with you?"

Of course Irene. It's your decision entirely.

I gather myself and attempt to shift the conversation away from my 'smalls' or, indeed, from my dad's 'bigs'! "So," I ask, "what time are you guys heading off?"

We'll wait until the world outside has drawn its curtains and hunkered down for the night. As such, we shall wait until midnight before departing.

"Coolio! 'Animals Do the Funniest Things' is on in ten minutes, let's watch that while we wait."

As you wish Irene though, I must say, the animals concerned do seem to lack our level of intelligence. That said, I do agree that there's little funnier than a skateboarding tortoise!

"Great idea guys!" I laugh as I click on the T.V.

And Irene, just one final thing before we settle down to watch this most amusing programme ... would you be so kind as to return the two necklaces and one fountain-pen that you appear to have 'acquired' since your arrival?

"Whoops! Soz babes. I didn't even know I'd done it! Looks like there's still a little way to go in my recovery! I certainly can't pull the wool over your eyes wonder dog – or even the cotton and polyester blend in the case of those pants."

Once my possessions have been returned, we companionably watch television until the clock strikes twelve. Despite my reservations and the swarm of butterflies in my stomach, I give Homes and Irene a big hug each, a thumbs-up and wish them on their way.

Even though I climb into bed, my plan is to force myself to stay awake until the two adventurers return but, somehow, sleep manages to wrap me in its arms and I drift away into a deep, dreamless, slumber.

Chapter 11

It's An Ill Wind That Blows!

I awake Saturday morning feeling fully refreshed! In fact, if it weren't for the note that I find stuck on the outside of my bedroom window explaining that Homes and Irene are being held captive, I'd have felt positively peachy!

The note reads:

Susan,

If you wish to see your vile hound and that ridiculous moggie again then come to Chalton Library at 10 am. Tell anyone and the animals get sliced up like a pair of baguettes!

I gasp! I imagine Homes and Irene, prisoners together, possibly afraid and definitely being really annoying to their captors!

I ease myself forward out of bed and prepare to hoist myself into my chair when I see a second note sitting squarely in the middle of my seat. "It's like working in a post office here!" I mutter as I grab the piece of paper. The type-face leaves me in no doubt as to the author ...

Dear Susan,

If you are reading these words then I have been captured. Do not be afraid, you must act calmly and do exactly as I say. Go out to the garden where you must shout 'It's time for 'Operation Big Jobs''. At this point, the preparations that I have been, painstakingly, making will spring into action.

Your faithful friend, Homes (lick mark)

I put my hand to my mouth, my wonderful Homes! "Get a grip Queen", I admonish myself, I have to act at once!

Clothes on, I speed out of the back door and into the garden. "I'm just getting a breath of fresh air," I call out to Mum who, fortunately, is the only other person in the house given that Dad is at work.

Once I reach the centre of the lawn I, slightly self-consciously, shout, "Time for 'Operation Big Jobs'!!"

I wait a few seconds with fear gnawing at my insides before I hear ...

"Message received and understood young lady. 'Operation Big Jobs' is a go lads! I repeat, 'Operation Big Jobs' is a go!"

With that, I hear a beating of wings and eight pigeons, in an arrow formation, fly over my head!

"Don't worry miss, we're all over it!" calls Wing Commander Peters from above, "Mr 'omes'll be back before you can say 'pigeon pie'!" I then hear snatches of conversation as the birds disappear into the distance ...

"Cor blimey sir, that's a bit close to the mark, I'm still 'avin nightmares!"

"Sorry S.C. I got over-excited!"

ooOOOOoo

Half an hour later, after rushing out of the front door, clutching Homes' tablet and shouting, "I'm just taking Homes for a quick walk!" I trundle up to the front doors of Chalton library which, as expected given that it's a Sunday, are firmly closed.

I sit facing the doors, a puzzled look on my face, until they, suddenly and ominously, slide open. I stare into the pit of darkness that lies beyond. "Here we go!" I think to myself as my arms propel me forward; past the books for sale, past the electronic machines for borrowing and renewing books and into the bowels of the library.

Aaaach, I'm suddenly blinded by light! My eyes adjust and I see there, in front of me, is Homes, lying on his side, back paws bound and tiny eyes flicking between me and Irene who lies to his right, three gruesome gashes in her side and a pool of crimson slowly growing around her. As I bend and slide his iPad towards him, I notice that Homes has a strange box strapped to his stomach and a trickle of blood running from beneath his left ear.

"Oh Homes!" I cry and start to move closer.

"I'm sorry dear, but no nearer I'm afraid," I hear a familiar voice command. I swivel my head and am confronted by a stern (yet fearful?) Ms Forbes. "You shouldn't have got involved dear! Look what's happened now!"

"I don't un ... understand ... " I stammer in bewilderment. My speech is interrupted by a clacking sound as Homes, gingerly, begins to type ...

Greetings Susan. I am afraid to say that Ms Jacqueline Forbes is not all that she seems. You see, Jacqueline, even when she was at school ... "

"Shut up!" screams Ms Forbes

... couldn't help ripping out those bewildering, bombastic, bottom burps that you always talk about, and that was why she was called ...

"Nooooooo!"

'Jacq ... the Ripper'!

Bewilderment turns to anger, "You!" I scream, "I trusted you Ms Forbes, I liked you ... a lot! You were always kind to me and yet you ... you are 'Jack the Ripper'! You do unspeakable things to animals ... and you film it!? You disgust me!"

"No, no ... " sobs Ms Forbes.

"Well, not really her Susan ... it was more ... " my head twists, again, to where, stepping out of deeper shadows appear Major Steel and Miss Hardcastle " ... us!"

Susan, allow me to introduce Major Steel, nickname 'Shovel' which, in rhyming slang, is 'shovel and spade' ... 'blade' given how he does like to slice things up! Alongside him is, of course, Miss Hardcastle, or 'Mousey' as she was known at school given how much she enjoyed killing small rodents!

"Oh so clever Mr Homes!" interjects Major Steel. "Myself and Mousey here take the animals, I slice the blighters up - you should hear them scream! – and Mousey films it all!"

"Pesky little animals," snickers Miss Hardcastle.

"And I watch them doing it! I sob my heart out seeing what's happening but still I distribute the DVDs to horrible, wretched people who like to view them – I disgust myself!!" bellows Ms Forbes.

"Well, you always were weak Jacqueline my girl, even at school. Always the victim, always doing what others said!" taunts the Major.

"I was afraid ... " mumbles Ms Forbes.

"That's no excuse!" I scream.

Bullies are bullies no matter what the age Susan and it's hard when you are alone with no friends to turn to.

"Oh, hark at the little doggie!" sneers Miss Hardcastle, "We had a good thing going until you had to interfere!"

"Calm yourself Mousey old girl," soothes Major Steel, "He'll get what's coming to him soon enough – just like that mouthy feline!

As Mousey said, it was a sweet deal until that twerp Robert took the wrong DVD. Fortunately, I was in your school for a governor's meeting, nabbed the old DVD and placed Miss Shakespeare's purse in Robert's bag and ... job done! A nice little distraction and frame-up – who'd ever believe anything that imbecile said!

But then you prod and you probe and then on Friday we watched your actions and heard you interrogate those gigantic, gormless Germans and then, to top it all, I received an email from our old school saying that someone had been making enquiries about us. As such, we knew it wouldn't take you much longer to put all of the pieces of our devious little puzzle together!

Still, I'm glad to see that you came alone Susan, as instructed. Frustratingly, you and your abominable animals clearly know too much about us and our operation and so, regrettably - in your case at least Susan - you will all have to die! The silver lining in this particular cloud, however, is that I see no need for anyone else to get hurt once you've been taken care of."

With a look of pure hatred the Major focuses his stare on Homes and adds, "Not so smart now are you scruff bag! You got captured here easy enough didn't you! The doors are all locked and there's no escape!"

Indeed, most unfortunate and something that would not have happened had the balaclava that I was wearing not slipped into my eyes causing me to topple off the desk into a waste-paper-basket! Irene should not have stayed to try to help me and I am distressed about her injuries. Still, I am confident that we will soon be rescued by ...

SMASH!

The library door shatters into a thousand fragments of sparkling glass as Dad crashes into the room followed by three, burly, police constables.

Excellent timing, the full weight of the law has arrived!

"Hold it right there Inspector!" snarls the Major, "Don't take another step or I'll blow us all into tiny pieces! I was an explosives expert in the army and that box, attached to our little canine friend, is a fiendish piece of equipment which will reduce us and half of Chalton to dust if I press this button!" With that, the Major holds aloft a device, about the size of a lighter, with a red button emerging ominously from its top.

"This device ... " he continues.

... Was diffused by me two hours ago.

"Impossible!" laughs the major, "It would take a genius to do such a thing!"

Precisely! It was child's play ... assuming that the child's parents were Albert Einstein and that nice lady on 'Countdown' who's really good at maths. As such, for me, it was a walk in the park ... which is where I need to be as soon as this fiasco is over – I have 'business' to attend to. Susan, I hope you've come equipped with a large bag!

"Curse you!" screams Major Steel, "I'll ... OOOOOOWWWWW! What in god's name was that?!"

"Wotcha Di!" I cry as my friend emerges from behind the Major whilst giving him a steely glare as she does so.

That's one spoon that won't be used in a kitchen again! So ...

Homes is cut off as, with a speed that belies her age, Miss Hardcastle grabs him and holds a glistening curved blade to his throat. "It may be the last thing I do, but I'm going to slit your throat from floppy ear to floppy ear you mangy excuse for a dog! You'll ... OOOOOUUUUFFFF!"

Miss Hardcastle's head snaps to the right as a punch lands plum on her jaw causing her knees to buckle and she falls to the floor like a sack of muddy potatoes.

"He may be a pompous, annoying, smug cross between a ferret and a dog, but he's family you old bag!" shouts Mum standing over Miss Hardcastle's prone form, "And I love him!"

And I am very fond of you too Rachel! Thank you for your timely intervention – you deserve a big drink tonight ... not that you wouldn't have had one anyway.

"Watch it, buster!" chuckles Mum.

I look to where Irene is lying and see that she is being gently lifted by a paramedic with Di holding one paw and whispering words of comfort. I hear "Bangin' boots babe" drift over from where they stand which gives me hope that with the tender mercies of a vet Irene will make a full recovery. I then scan round to where Ms Forbes sits alone, on a chair, gently weeping. Homes, now freed, and I move over to her.

"At school," she mutters, glassy-eyed and hands trembling, "it was 'Ripper' this and 'Ripper' that. I leave school but the two of them just carry on ... 'oohh, did you hear her fart', 'wow, that was a top trump', 'blimey, there's a blistering bottom burp' ... I just can't take it anymore!"

I try to reassure her with, "It's over now Ms Forbes, no one will be making hurtful remarks to do with ... you know ... anymore."

Indeed. Not since I realised that something didn't smell right and got wind of what was going on.

"Homes!" I murmur.

The whole scheme has backfired horribly. At least now you can put it all behind you.

"Oooohh!" sobs Ms Forbes.

We leave Ms Forbes with a policeman who needs to take a statement before escorting her to the police station.

And, with that, Homes, Mum, Dad and I, hugging, laughing and crying all at the same time, make our way outside.

We see Major Steel being helped into the back of a police van and, like all villains, he can't resist leaving without a final flourish. He fixes his eyes on me and snarls, "I may not be able to walk away from this young lady, but at least I can walk which is more than you'll ever be able to do!"

"Then again, she can sit down which is more than you can do with a spoon wedged up your ... ." begins Dad.

"AAAAAAAARRRRRRGGGGGGGHHHHHH!!!!" screams the Major before Dad manages to complete his profanity, "I'm blind!"

"That's one in the eye for you guv!" comes a voice from above, "That's me special blackberry and nettle surprise!"

"Ohhh, it stings!!"

"That's nettles for you! Just isn't your lucky day is it!"

"Nice one S.C" I cry, looking to the heavens.

"Me pleasure miss, think of it as a present from the lads!" he chortles as his wings take him up and away from us, off, no doubt, to spread a little more luck and create a steady stream of business for Chalton's two dry cleaning shops!

Chapter 12

New Beginnings

Six days later and we're gathered in Robbie's front room. The week has been a never ending series of police statements, phone calls and general discussions. Now here we all were:

1. Myself and Homes, who has fully recovered from the minor injuries that had been inflicted upon him. The two of us are firmly back in Mum and Dad's good books and, in fact, have been treated like returning heroes ever since 'The Mysterious Case of the Mysterious Case', as Homes likes to refer to it, reached its thrilling conclusion.

2. Di and Irene. Irene is still recovering, but seems to have 'bonded' with Di and, as such, she now calls Di's home her 'crib'! Apparently they are getting on famously and are thoroughly enjoying talking nail polish and playing 'hunt the tiara'!

3. Robbie, now fully re-instated in school, along with his present from his mum and dad ... a massive Irish wolfhound, who Robbie is struggling to think of a name for. Homes and the wolfhound seem to be hitting it off famously - that's if the good natured barks and sniffing are anything to go by. They may look like a mouse sitting next to a pony but they certainly appear to be becoming firm friends!

"So, let me get this right," Robbie is saying, "you alerted Wing Commander Peters and S.C. Suz and they ... "

" ... Plus the other lads," I explain, "dropped a message that Homes had written for my dad. He then leapt into action by calling in help from extra policemen and phoning my mum who rushed to the library and grabbed Di on the way.

Dad reckons that Major Steel and Miss Hardcastle will be put away for the rest of their lives. He also says that they discovered a concealed room, or 'chamber of death' as he put it, at the back of the library where The Major and Miss Hardcastle carried out their vile acts and where they forced Ms Forbes to watch what they did. Loads of people who paid to watch the DVDs have been arrested."

"Wow, it's amazing," continues Robbie. "This cruelty and making money from selling those disgusting films had been going on for years until I come along and expose the whole thing!"

Well, I think you'll find ...

"Spot on, Rob!" I laugh, winking at Homes.

"You're a hero Robster!" cries Di. "That said, I am interested to understand how Homes came to suspect the Major and Miss Hardcastle?"

Aha! Once I realised that the DVD and, as such, the library was key I suspected that it must be the main distribution point for the evil films. This fitted with my map which showed that Chalton was the spider sitting firmly at the centre of the web of crimes which appear to have been committed over a wide area for many years – they began miles away from us but, over time, have been moving ever closer to Chalton village.

And when I learned Ms Forbes Christian name and heard (and smelt!) certain bodily functions, I thought that we had found our 'Ripper'!

We must then turn our attention to the Major and Miss Hardcastle. Their nicknames and the information that I ascertained from their old school 'sealed the deal' as the saying goes but they really gave themselves away when I lay on the library floor and presented my stomach for rubbing - did they take the opportunity to do so? No, they did not! To ignore a dog as obviously lovable and attractive as me marked them out as very dubious characters indeed - they clearly held some form of deep-seated hatred of animals!

"Exactimo!" cooes Irene. "No normal people could ignore my handsome, hench, Homesey!"

"Who are we talking about now?" enquires Robbie. "I don't know any hand ... "

"Anyway," I interrupt, "the villains have got what they deserve, at last. What I just can't understand though, and maybe I never will, is what drove The Major and Miss Hardcastle to behave the way that they did – I didn't believe that demons really existed until now!" As I speak I, unexpectedly, find tears running down my face like whispers against my skin.

Homes pushes himself up against me, his fur a welcome comfort as I watch him type …

Some things we may never understand Susan. Was evil always within them? Were they simply not given enough love as children? Did some particular event set them on their villainous path? Who knows? What I do know, however, is that, for all of the bad people in the world, there are many more wonderful and kind ones and where there is evil, there are people (and animals too!) who will do all that they can to ensure that it does not prevail. People and animals like us!

"True." replies Robbie, as I give Homes a massive squeeze, "I'm upset about Ms Forbes though. I know what it's like to be bullied, so I hope she won't be treated too harshly. Still Suz, your dad says that because she's shown real remorse and was forced to do what she did under a dress ... "

Under duress.

"Ah, right, under duress. Yeah, anyway, because of that they'll look to just get her to do some community service. So, it's all turned out well in the end," finishes Robbie, turning on the T.V. "Let's see if there's anything good on that we can all watch."

"Woof!" barks the wolfhound.

"Nothing on there," says Robbie, "let's try another channel."

"Woof!" barks the wolfhound again.

After Robbie has changed the channel a further six times with this being punctuated by his new dog barking each time, I ask Homes to translate.

Simple Susan, he enjoys watching television and is simply asking 'what's on?'

"Well I never!" giggles Robbie, "He always does that! I think I've found a name for him then! I'm going to call him 'Whatson'! Ha!"

"Sounds good," I whisper dreamily, as I settle back in my chair ... "Homes and Whatson ... it has a certain ring to it don't you think?"

THE END

Printed in Great Britain
by Amazon